ALWAYS ALERT

Anstruther and his three cronies were clever and quick. They almost toppled Fox before he was aware. But Fox was always alert. By ducking and twisting sideways, he was able to stick out a hard leg and trip the first ruffian. He put a fist into the guts of number two, swiveled, and kicked number three. Number one was on his feet again but bent over like a fool. Fox kicked him in the face. He went over backwards, spraying the remnants of bone, gristle, and blood from a smashed nose.

Fox jumped for Anstruther, striking him—twice. First in the stomach, then bringing his knee up so that Anstruther's large and generous mouth squashed bloodily.

"Listen, you whoreson! I am not some chicken to be plucked. You try anything else, Anstruther, and I'll break your arms off," snarled Fox. With a final kick at Anstruther's head, Fox rolled off to his just bed.

THE FOX SERIES

#1 THE PRESS GANG

#2 PRIZE MONEY

#3 SAVAGE SIEGE

#4 TREASURE MAP

#5 SAILOR'S BLOOD

#6 SEA OF GOLD

#7 COURT MARTIAL

#8 BATTLE SMOKE

#9 CUT AND THRUST

FOX: CUT AND THRUST
BY ADAM HARDY

PINNACLE BOOKS • NEW YORK CITY

This is a work of fiction. All the characters and events portrayed in this book are fictional, and any resemblance to real people or incidents is purely coincidental.

FOX: CUT AND THRUST

Copyright © 1974 by Adam Hardy

All rights reserved, including the right to reproduce this book or portions thereof in any form.

A Pinnacle Books edition, published by special arrangement with New English Library, Limited, London.

ISBN: 0-523-00673-X

First printing, July 1975

Printed in the United States of America

PINNACLE BOOKS, INC.
275 Madison Avenue
New York, N.Y. 10016

CUT AND THRUST

CHAPTER ONE

"Mr. Fox! Damme, sir! What kind of nonsense is this?"

Captain Percy Staunton waved the sheet of paper in Fox's face, glaring up all pop-eyed and chinless, his smooth face scarlet, gobbling his rage.

"My report of the recent action, sir."

Fox had spent some time on that report, sitting in his cabin which, as befitted the first lieutenant of an eighty gun ship of the line, obtruded considerably more upon the deck space around the bulk of a thirty-two-pounder than the cabins of the other lieutenants. Fox had written enough reports in his time to comprehend the jargon, the laconic navalese, the phrases of dry prose that concealed the smash and crash of the broadsides, with the brown smoke gushing, and the grape whickering across the decks and degutting and decapitating, and splattering those white decks with blood.

"Your report! Goddammit, Mr. Fox, I know that!"

"I merely reported what occurred."

Captain Staunton pushed back from his desk and stood

up. His affable flap-eared face appeared as wrathful as ever Fox remembered it. He stuck his hands up under the tails of his coat and with his head thrust down so as not to strike his head against the overhead—on the eighty-gun ship of the line *Hector* an unnecessary gesture—he stalked up and down the black and yellow painted canvas checkerboard. Fox regarded his captain with that ugly visage of his as excited as a lump of stone. For once, Fox felt at a loss. He wondered just what it was that was so exercising our Percy.

"See here, Mr. Fox." Staunton swung his arms from behind his back with a great crackle of Fox's paper. He stabbed a stiff forefinger down. "See here. Do you or do you not, sir, state here: 'The line then tacked together and so secured the weather gage'?"

"Yes, sir."

"But do you state *how* that was accomplished?"

"The facts are there. They speak for themselves—"

"Goddammit, Mr. Fox! *I* know! *You* know! But will anyone reading this know it was you who gave the orders that secured us the weather gage? And, see here: '. . . thus the five sternmost ships of the enemy line were brought to action in such a way that the two foremost were unable to come to their assistance.' You do not say how that was done."

Fox shook his head. "You asked me to write a report so that the admiral might avail himself of the information—"

"Quite so, sir! Quite so! Admiral Cloughton was sick and stuffed below in the orlop. You and I know I rely in everything absolutely upon you, Mr. Fox. You, sir, it was who carried four of His Majesty's ships into a glorious action with seven of the enemy—and outwitted 'em—lay me horizontal, Mr. Fox!—blew up two, took three, and made the other two run! Goddammit, Mr. Fox! Don't you un-

2

derstand what it was you did?" And all Percy Staunton's youthful enthusiastic glowing face beamed in the remembered glory.

George Abercrombie Fox knew all about glory. Glory was reserved for the gold-laced big-wigs who had nothing better to think about. He had a ship under him which had been knocked about, and he had a crew to remind of their duty, and he had this captain who, affable and puppy-friendly though he might be, was still a scion of the nobility and therefore an object of derision, and he had, also, an admiral who was dangerously and maniacally ill to chart a course for through the shoals of naval politics.

"I think the admiral was pleased with what we did."

Percy Staunton started to pace again, changed his mind, threw the paper onto his desk and then slumped into his chair. He glared up at Fox, and, again, Fox could not remember having seen our Percy so exalted before, not, oddly, even in the midst of action.

"I shall pass this report on to Admiral Cloughton, Mr. Fox. Before I do that I shall make a few additions." He kept his protruding eyes fixed on Fox's ugly face. "And I shall brook no objections from you, Mr. Fox . . . Just remember that I *am* the captain of this ship."

Fox nodded. That was the second time Staunton had indicated that, sometimes, he realized that he was the captain.

"Very good, sir." He was about to go on, in his own ugly way, when with the briefest of knocks upon the door and a great rushing swoop, Midshipman Gruber burst in.

"Please sir!" Gruber said, and here, at least, any pretence at who actually ran the ship was set aside, for the midshipman spoke directly to Fox, here, in the captain's cabin. "Mr. Carker's compliments, sir, and can you come?"

3

Fox, about to bellow a foul and cutting reprimand at the boy, halted as Gruber babbled on: "It's Colum, sir— he's gone mad!"

Paddy Colum, the captain of the foretop, had always been a quiet and steady man. Able to hand, reef and steer, a volunteer, he was an Irishman for whom Fox had always had approval. In the recent battle Colum had fought well. Fox pushed smartly past Gruber and the marine sentry, who stiffened into a human ramrod at sight of that ugly black bastard Fox, and hared for the quarterdeck. If Carker had sent for him, it meant trouble, for the good Carker had sailed with Fox long enough now to know his ways. And, too, Fox had sailed with John Carker long enough to know that Carker, who was the seventh lieutenant of the ship—although that would alter!—would never send for him unless the situation was almost past retrieval.

Without pausing and yet instinctively and almost without being aware of his actions, Fox looked about the horizons, up at the criss-crossing maze of rigging, at the masts and yards, and he felt the wind on his cheek and the feel of the ship through the sea and, instantly, was in full command of all the information any sailorman must have at his finger tips.

Able seaman Colum stood straddle-legged on the gangway. His hand held a cocked pistol. His right slashed a cutlass about in vicious yet aimless curves, as though he was still caught up in a frenzy of action. At his feet and half-off the gangway lay the body of the master at arms. The man's head had been crushed in and blood and brains dripped greasily down onto the deck beneath, between two of the twenty-four-pounders. Fox felt the instant wrath of any first lieutenant at seeing his precious white holystoned decks being marked in any way.

Lieutenant Quilley approached the frenzied figure of

4

Colum with a catlike grace. Quilley, an officer with a lightness about him, who liked to quote Homeric verse, kept his intense gaze fixed on the mad seaman.

Colum was mad. Oh, yes, everyone in the whole Royal Navy was mad, Fox knew that. But their madnesses were contained and controlled and could be observed only in silly, stupid, almost farcical eccentricities. Now Colum had been tipped over the invisible brink into this ghastly madness that had done to death the master at arms. Fox had no love for the men who occupied that loveless position aboard; but someone had to police the ships of the navy, and with their ship's corporals, the masters at arms undertook the thankless task for the extra rewards it brought.

Carker swung around to Fox.

"I can see, Mr. Carker."

Fox had seized the situation at once, and did not want anything to detract from the efforts Mr. Quilley, the third of the ship, was making.

He felt that the best thing to do in these circumstances would be to hurl a belaying pin at the madman. But Quilley was now almost up to Colum. Quilley held out his hand.

"That pistol and cutlass should have been returned as soon as the action finished." Quilley spoke not with the habitual intolerant rasp of an officer addressing one of the hands, rather, he spoke in the wheedling way a man might speak to a pet dog who held his slippers between his jaws and would not give them up. "Hand them over now, Colum, like a sensible fellow."

His Britannic Majesty's eighty gun ship of the line *Hector* heeled in a smooth rhythmical surging to the breeze blowing across her larboard quarter. She was on the larboard tack and heading up into the north east, heading back to England and home, with her crew depleted by action, with her sides plugged with shot cones, with much of her fabric wounded and many of her spars still suspect. But she presented a familiar sight to any seaman, with the creak of the rigging and the heave and groan of timbers, the rush and chuckle of the wash overside.

Fox knew Colum was not hearing or seeing these familiar things.

Colum was seeing the livid faces of men choked in death, the belching clouds of smoke and the darting tongues of flame as the guns roared; he was hearing the horrible whicker and whine of roundshot passing above, and the smashing crash of falling spars and the rattle of blocks pelting down from above. He was seeing men caught up in combat. And he was re-living all these things on the gangway, with a pistol and a cutlass, and with the dead body of the master at arms at his feet.

Silence held everyone gripped in a tight expectation.

Only the calm gentle voice of Lieutenant Quilley, wheedling, coaxing, lifted in that uncanny silence.

"You'd best be taking a rest, Colum. Off watch. Go below." Quilley advanced further, his undress uniform as smart and clean as it always was, blue and white and brave under the weak Atlantic sunshine. *Hector* heeled and everyone in the ship slanted automatically with that heel and so rode the ship's movements and swayed back the other way.

"Sink you for a rascally Froggie!" Colum screamed the words out, and now flecks of foam splattered from his split lips. "I'll do for you!"

"Now, now, Colum! You know me! I'm Mr. Quilley, and you know what'll happen if you don't obey your orders! You're a fine seaman, Colum. Don't spoil all that now."

"Fire and blood!" shrieked Colum, verbalizing at last the horrors he had kept tightly battened down during the action, remembered horrors now bursting over the barriers of his reason. "Goddamm you to hell, you Froggie bastard!"

And he struck out with the cutlass and cleft down through Mr. Quilley's face.

Quilley dropped, spouting blood, and his fine and neat and impeccable uniform showed now the colors of red, white and blue.

"My God!" The horrified exclamation burst out from Captain Staunton's ashen lips. He had walked through onto the quarterdeck in time to witness this act that was so outrageous that, aboard a British man of war, it was inconceivable.

Fox did not waste time cursing. He was aware of the enormity of his sin of omission. Here he had been standing here and letting Quilley get on with this job in the way Quilley, being the kind of man he was, had thought best. All Quilley's character had been displayed in that gentle approach, the attempt at reason; the great Homeric laughter that must now be gusting up from wherever flame pit of hell Quilley had gone would be the louder in ironic self-contempt.

Fox would have gone in—bash, bash—but he had held a growing respect for Quilley that had nothing to do with what he must do now.

Carker said: "I'll get the bastard, sir—"

"No, Mr. Carker! You'll vastly oblige me by not getting yourself killed."

Captain Staunton hovered. "We must do something, Mr. Fox. God knows what our consorts will be thinking."

These few words took perhaps a heartbeat or two—and then Fox had taken a swift run along the gangway, letting

7

Staunton's words float into the air, and he bunched his leg muscles and felt his blood thumping as he dived with all his hard and compact body driving behind the tackle. He took Colum around the waist with his left hand. His right arm shot up and his knuckles, as seamed, as brown, as hard, as the old English oak from which the heart would be selected for the toughest constructions of a ship of the line, smashed into Colum's jaw. The descending cutlass blow whirled over Fox's back and the cutlass swung and dangled uselessly from its sword knot around Colum's wrist.

Fox gave a vicious intemperate squeeze with his left arm and shoulder, although Colum was already unconscious, and made sure of the man, and, stepping back, let the seaman slump to the gangway.

What Staunton had said made sense.

Astern of *Hector* followed *Sheringham, Bridchester* and *Tyrian.* The two prizes also wallowed along in the wake. One had sunk, the seventy-four that had been opposed to *Sheringham,* and had thus compounded the mischief she had begun with her fierce resistance to Captain Peter Gale's seventy-four *Sheringham,* and·continued with her refusal to strike before the arrival of three units of the Channel Fleet led by the ninety-eight *Tiger.*

"See to Colum, Mr. Carker. Speak to the ship's corporal personally, mind."

"Aye aye, sir."

Carker would know what exactly to do in these circumstances.

Fox walked rapidly back to the quarterdeck, turned to face forward, half leaning against the rail. He stared along the deck, up toward the forecastle where the bell hung, past the crowded faces of the men in the waist and along the forrard ends of the gangways.

George Abercrombie Fox just looked.

Instantly, without a word being spoken, the hands resumed their work, with the bosun's mates walking among them ready with their colts. Mr. Gold, the master, was speaking to Staunton, and the ship heaved across the sea and resumed her usual routine; but for the moment Fox let all that familiar world slide out of his mind. He could see what that poor devil Colum had been seeing. He understood the demons that drove a man.

Mind you, there was no time for pity or compassion in this man's navy.

Those were emotions that got you where Quilley was now.

Fox could also see that other emotions, those, for instance, harbored habitually by the master at arms, had also brought that devious man to the same place as Quilley.

Fox already knew, and this day's work merely confirmed his belief, that you had to steer a middling course between those two sets of extreme emotions.

The routine of the ship would continue, for everyone aboard, every single human soul, knew that Lieutenant Fox would not tolerate imperfection, or slovenliness, or slackness, and that although no one had been flogged since the very early days of *Hector's* commission, there would be as many red checked shirts at the gangways as were necessary to bring the ship up to the standard that Lieutenant Fox required.

Mr. Gold, the master, made the observation that perhaps he, alone, might venture without being crudely snubbed. Fox knew that John Carker would not venture, and Staunton would take a very different view. As for Black Dick Cloughton, the admiral beneath whose flag they sailed, he lay in his cot coughing and choking, with a face like a purple plum, his eyes starting from his head—and his hand not to be prized from the brandy bottle.

"Had Colum been shot down where he stood, Mr. Fox, he would have been spared much agony."

"So he would." Fox considered. "So he would, Mr. Gold."

"By exercising mercy in taking him alive, Mr. Fox, he has been saved for a worse fate."

Fox supposed, with the deep and dark side of his nature, that he had realized this at the time, and had not acknowledged it. A marine could have been told to shoot Colum. Fox could have pistolled the poor devil's brains out himself. One thing was for sure, G. A. Fox wouldn't miss.

But he had not done either of these things. He had jumped in and saved Colum for the torture that was to come.

Perhaps, seeing Quilley lying there with his handsome face a cleft and bloody ruin, all these things had gone through Fox's head. He had understood what he had been doing. Perhaps. Perhaps it had all been as instinctive as he had believed it.

But he knew, too, that he could not feel any remorse that he had prevented Colum from taking the easy way out and being shot there and then. He could not pretend he felt any sorrow that the man would be hanged from the yardarm.

Damn Colum!

Mr. Quilley had been a promising officer. And—suppose it had been John Carker who had fallen to the gangway with his face slashed off?

G. A. Fox would not even think of that possibility.

G. A. Fox was growing old and senile, that was for sure. He went roaring into the crew, making every last little

10

detail of the ship as perfect as any ship might ever be in this world after she had gone through an action. He shouted and cursed and damned and blinded and very soon he could regard his inward images of Quilley's faceless corpse, and Colum in irons under the halfdeck, as merely past incidents in his hectic career at sea.

Hector, proudly flying the flag of Rear-Admiral of the Blue, Sir Richard Cloughton, and followed by *Sheringham*, Captain Peter Gale, *Bridchester*, Captain John Presford and *Tyrian*, Captain William Bowness, sailed grandly up Channel.

The four ships made a gorgeous spectacle with the sun gleaming from their saffron sails, the water foaming whitely past, their flags all a stiff flutter. Superbly handled, they came around, like machines tacking together, read· for the professional approach to their moorings that w. the hallmark of captains and crews who were complete masters of their ships and—certainly not masters,—more lovers in hatred and affection for their mistress the sea. Fox stood on the quarterdeck of the flagship and watched with both his eyes brilliant and intemperate as the evolutions were carried out and the crew scampered aloft and the canvas came in and the ship settled, with almost an audible sigh, into the comparative quiescence of moorings.

"Mr. Fox," said Captain Staunton. He looked magnificent in his gold lace and full dress uniform. "I have taken the liberty I mentioned to you previously and your report has gone in with mine to the admiral, for his private use. What he will say in his letter to the Admiralty I do not know." Here Staunton gave again a strange flashing glimpse of the man that lived inside his nincompoopish exterior. "But, damme, sir, I know what that report should be!"

"We brought back but two prizes. And *Tiger* and her

11

two consorts came up whilst *Sheringham* was still fighting." Fox felt bitter about that.

"Captain Gale no doubt will have an excellent explanation, particularly as his opponent subsequently sank. But, I agree, Mr. Fox, it is an unfortunate occurrence."

"Too damn right," said Fox with no attempt at grace.

Just because three ships of the line had hove up within sight and sound of the battle before the action was over, so that the guns had still been roaring as they approached, meant that *Tiger, Defence* and *Elephant* would take their shares of what prize money was going. The rule was the rule. However unfair it might seem, it was naval custom.

"Anyway, the two prizes look to be in worse shape than we could wish for. They'll be hulked, for sure."

"You should get a little gold out of it, Mr. Fox." And then Staunton recognized his gaffe, and swung away, and Fox went uglily forward to check up on the forecastle. Carker would have done everything perfectly, of course; but Fox would not let that halt him from displaying his bad temper.

He was a jumped up marsh boy from the Thames, who had come up through the hawsehole onto the quarterdeck, and to him money was what the navy was all about—or almost all about. Staunton had money worries of a kind quite different and removed from those which gave Fox such enormous problems.

"Very good, Mr. Carker." Then, weakly, Fox added: "It seems this is the end of another commission, Mr. Carker."

"Yes, sir." Carker hesitated, then added: "I could have wished it to have been longer. And it's ending with a court martial and a hanging."

Fox looked at the good Carker. He needed money as much as Fox did. They had been through a very great

12

deal together. Being made had done something to Carker; he had been made in ways that had nothing to do with the King's commission he had received, and his whole attitude reflected the newness of the joy in him at his good fortune. Fox, sourly, reflected that he had felt genuine pleasure that Carker had been given his commission. Carker and Grey—he still did not know which one had received his commission first and thereby remained forever senior to the other. Rather, not forever, for Grey would almost certainly be posted very soon, before Fox himself, in all probability, and Carker's chances were as slim as Fox's own.

Then, looking at John Carker, and remembering where he was and what had happened, Fox had to pause with a genuine shock. He was the first lieutenant of the flagship. They had just fought a highly successful action. Oh, surely, the prizes were small and there would be little prize money, and he had been blinded by that. But—he had to face what he had been unwilling to face. There would be rewards, promotions, swords of honor. There would almost certainly be a swab in it for the first lieutenant of the flagship, surely? Promotion of a captain's first lieutenant was taken as a compliment to the captain.

Could it be that George Abercrombie Fox, at last, would receive his step, wear a gilt swab on his left shoulder, swagger in all the glory of *Commander* Fox?

God knew, he had done enough to be Admiral of the Red, in his time.

Could it be?

Could it . . . ?

CHAPTER TWO

The fat little book had been sumptuously bound in a rich leather binding, with gold tooling, and the gold had dulled to a deep ochre tinge, whilst the crimson of the leather, much rubbed and scuffed, glowed with a deeper luster. Fox held the book in his hands, standing on the almost deserted quarterdeck of *Hector*, and turned the cover.

On the flyleaf, written in the impeccable hand of a scholar, the name: William Lovelace Quilley, and the date, 1st of June, 1793. Quilley had been about twenty-four or so when he'd been killed, so he'd had this book given to him at seventeen. At that age Fox had been years at sea: at that date he'd been engaged in the opening phases of the present war. Would the damn'd war never end? But, if it did, then also would end all his chances of promotion and prize.

He turned the title page.

'Twenty-four Bookes of Homer's Odisses'

That was a lie, for the book contained only those parts of Homer's story that Quilley had particularly loved, and

14

he had no doubt had those sections bound up just because he was fascinated by Chapman's famous and justly renowned translation. Fox felt the warm limp softness of the book between his fingers. Poor Quilley!

Like any sensible man Quilley had made a will before action and, to everyone's surprise and most of all to Fox's own, there, plainly to be read, was stated that Quilley wished his small copy of Chapman's Homer—or these parts of the story—to go to Lieutenant Fox. The bequest was a codicil. The full text of Homer in Greek which Quilley doted on would go back with his effects to his home in Hampshire where a sorrowing father might touch the pages and think of the son he had lost.

Gulls screeched past overhead, their heads down, their eyes bright, their cruel sharp beaks waiting to snap up whatever might offer. A light breeze blew from the south west, and a few high clouds scudded. The warming sun shone bravely on the dockyard and the water and the crowds of boats, on the surrounding hills where trees were coming fully into leaf. Life had to go on, even if a young man of promise was so stupidly dead.

For the death of Mr. Morrill, master at arms of *Hector*, and of Lieutenant Quilley, third of the ship, Able Seaman Colum had stood his court martial and had been duly hanged. Now *Hector* was being readied to move into dry dock, her masts drawn by the sheer hulk, her officers paid off with the exception of her standing officers and a few master's mates who, with Fox, would deal with the last details. Captain Staunton, too, was still aboard; but he was due to go to his father's country estate in Sussex on the morrow. He had been greatly kind to Fox, as had Admiral Cloughton in his gruff and chokey way. Cloughton had posted hot foot to Whitehall. Fox wished the old bastard well of his famous victory, that men were now calling

Cloughton's Action, and could not stop himself from a tenseness he despised over what might very soon transpire.

The men of *Hector* had not been paid off. As was the usual custom they had been packed off to a receiving ship and from thence would be assigned new ships. For a brief space they might play merry hell, with the garlands draping their ships, and their doxies aboard with what rum or liquor they might smuggle aboard between their breasts or clamped to their massive thighs, and the tween decks would resemble all the horrors unimaginable to a landsman.

Fox closed the book. He was a devoted follower of Molière and of François Villon, both after Shakespeare, of course; but he would treasure this Homer of Quilley's.

There was some news that reached him to cheer him up, resolute as he was against any premature hopes for his own future. Nelson, who had taken the penultimate ship of Napoleon's ill-fated Egyptian fleet, had at last succeeded in taking them all. *Le Genereux* had been taken on 18th February, and the news, the glorious news, was that Nelson in Palermo had sent his flagship *Foudroyant* commanded by Sir Edward Berry back to Malta just in time to take *Le Guillaume Tell* as that ship attempted to escape. So all the ships anchored in the Bay of Aboukir had been taken. Fox cursed that he had had no part in that great and glorious action, stuck so ignominiously fast in *Culloden* on that goddamned sandbank; but for the sake of Nelson he rejoiced. Mind you, he had had his ideas of Fox—the Charles James, the politician, of that illustrious name—severely shaken by the reports of Fox's attack on Nelson, over a pack of pesky rebels in the Bay of Naples. Fox—the George Abercrombie of that ilk—knew well enough that only a fool believed what the newspapers said, and the leaden prints fabricated allusions and half-truths to suit their own purposes. But, all the same, being a one-time hot-head of the L.C.S. and a serving officer of the Royal Navy were apparently incompatible roles for a single man.

Being G. A. Fox and with a family of Foxes by the Thames to support, he knew where his bread and butter came from—rather his hard tack.

He could recall his savage delight when he'd first come across stories of old Luke Foxe—who called himself North-West Foxe—in connection with Frobisher and Hudson and Baffin and the search for the North West Passage. Foxe used an 'e' at the end of his name; but G. A. F. knew what he knew. Luke Foxe was a commoner, a nothing, a man like Fox himself, of humble origins, as the cant phrase had it, and he had fought and bashed and struggled his way up in life.

There was a Fox Strait leading off north westwards from Hudson Bay.

Well, who knew? What might not the cartographers insert in their charts in the future? Back five years, in 1795, the Admiralty had seen fit to appoint a Hydrographer, and Fox was in the mood to give him some work to do.

The feeling of a ship in *Hector's* condition always came strangely to Fox. The ship lay in the water, loglike, her masts gone, her people gone, her very spirit, it seemed, vanished. Soon they'd warp her up and then, once she was berthed tightly and snugly, Fox could take himself off. There would be very few people who would care where he went or what he did; despite the toll of war and the commissioning of new ships, there were always plenty of able lieutenants grasping for appointments.

Years of sourness could not be thrown off lightly.

Fox looked up as a strange procession came aboard. He

17

stood on that deserted quarterdeck—and how typical of Fox it was that he should choose to stand on the quarterdeck when he had a whole empty ship in which to roam. Staunton would soon be gone; he was reading his letters at this moment.

Leading that incongruous procession came a very large, very fat, very black man clad in all the gorgeousness of Oriental robes and turban and feathers, with slippers that, as Fox recalled in memory of Ibrahim who had brought the harem aboard *Clothilde*, curled up at the tips. But this man's clothes were no wrecked refuse from a shipwreck. He sparkled in the early sunshine. And, following him, the others of the group sparkled resplendently also. They formed a guard, and they carried scimitars, and they were clad as the Turks Fox had known in Acre had been clad, except that here the jewels, the silks, the richness, the lavishness of Turkish show dazzled and delighted.

The man for whom this procession formed both guard and badge of rank moved forward and, with a small but effectively powerful motion of his hand, sent the guards back across the quarterdeck. Fox did not move. No British sea officer would move on his own quarterdeck for anyone less than another British sea officer of superior rank. Fox stood there and waited, calmly, knowing that no jackanapes troupe of Turkish odd-bodies could possibly make its way through Plymouth dockyards and aboard a ship of His Britannic Majesty through guards and marines without every assistance to be afforded by the Navy itself.

The man gave Fox a quick and searching glance. He was not over-tall, but well-built and, at probably only forty or so, was already running to fat. His robes, his jewels, his turban were all of the most expensive, and his face showed a jaded appetite for the fleshpots of life, and a

18

faded lust after all that absolute power within his own house and harem could afford. Contrasting him with Mustafa Murad, that beardless and ferociously active janissary, a chorbaji of the jemaat, with whom Fox had shared adventures in the Mediterranean and with whom, also, he had created that bawdy jest circulating in the navy,—Oh, yes,—Fox remembered things Turkish with very mixed emotions! He had fought the good fight at Acre, with Sir Sidney Smith, and they had beaten back the mad Corsican bandit Bonaparte. And Fox had used Chorbaji Murad's men in his attack on the old *Maria*, when Fox's Patent Brothel for Boarding First Rates had first seen the light of day.

Now this man bowed—not deeply, enough to indicate he was being merely formal—and he spoke in an English that although accented was clear and good enough for anyone.

"I have the honor to address Captain Fox?"

Fox grimaced—and cursed for that silly weakness.

"I am Lieutenant Fox." About to go on he was harshly interrupted.

"It is Captain Fox I wish to see. Please convey my compliments at once. I have no time to waste."

Now was no time to explode in anger.

A bunch of yammering heathens coming aboard a King's ship and one of them putting on airs and trying to give orders!

"Captain Staunton is still in the ship—"

"Captain Fox, you witless loon! By—" And here the Turk ripped off an interesting string of Arabic oaths that Fox followed reasonably faithfully, having served with the Turks and having picked up the stickier portions of the language.

19

No British officer was going to stand for that sort of nonsense!

"Tell me what you want aboard my ship, you blagskite, or I'll have you in the bilboes and all your men with you! Sink me! I've served with Turks who'd cut you up and fry your liver for breakfast! Spit it out, you whore-son spavined dog or I'll knock your teeth out!"

The man halted his lurid cursing and hung there with open mouth. He took a step backwards. He glared at Fox.

Then—then he smiled! His face broke into a delighted smile and he chuckled, and said: "You are as I have been informed. The Chorbaji Murad did not speak false. You are Captain Fox."

Fox understood now.

"I was when the chorbaji and I—"

"Quite so. If you are a lieutenant now the British have a strange way of rewarding their faithful servants."

There was no answer to that.

"Unless it is the women you have been at again, as the good Yassin Soliman informs me was your habitual custom at Acre."

"Yassin Soliman! He still lives, then? I am overjoyed to hear it. I feared the plague—"

"He has not favored me with all your doings—there was a story of a harem being disturbed one night—no proof—but—"

It was Fox's turn to interrupt.

"And his wife? His family?"

"They all live. The plague mercifully did not kill them, all praise to Allah the all wise the all merciful."

Fox it was who had cut the buboes from the armpits and the groins of the women, cutting in with his knife, seeing the green and black pus spouting, holding them down as they raved. That had been a desperate night's

20

work. And now this Turk had news of Yassin Soliman of Acre, who had been high in the favors—such as they were —of the Butcher, Djezzar Pasha, the Lord of Acre, and word also from the Chorbaji Murad, who had sworn he would not forget G. A. Fox.

"I am Murad Ali—" Fox stopped listening after the first half dozen names and titles rolled out. Murad was a name he could get to grips with. "As I have said, I have little time. I must report to London, where my command of English is required." Fox could only wonder at what new schemes were being cooked up between the British government and the Porte and guessed something must be brewing in the Mediterranean once more. He'd like to serve out there again some time. He'd had some fine rousing times out in the Med, that was for sure.

"A new Order has been instituted by the grand Signor, as you are probably knowing, and the great Lord Nelson has been honored as the first receptor." Murad's English was beginning to break down; and Fox tried to put a less demoniac glare on his ugly face. Poor Murad seemed quite discomposed by it, for he had studiously refrained from looking into Fox's face after that first occasion when he had seen clearly enough he was dealing with the man he had been ordered to see.

"The Order of the Crescent," said this Murad. "Begun by the Grand Signor personally. Lord Nelson has already received his star, for he has served us well." Fox had heard what Nelson had received from the Turks, and, like Nelson, valued the chelengk, the jewelled aigrette to be worn in his hat. This star, now, this was something new. "The brother of Sir Sidney Smith, in Constantinople, Spencer Smith, has designed the star. You have been honored, Capt—Lieutenant Fox, to receive the star of the Order of the Crescent."

Fox just gaped.

A massive eunuch stepped forward with a sandalwood box. It revealed, nestling on a satin cushion, a glittering sparkling scintillating star, with at its center a star and a crescent. The thing looked impossible, there on the quarterdeck of a British ship of the line. Yet it was real. Murad lifted it out and there and then fastened it to Fox's coat. Fox could not move a muscle. He just stood there like the loon he was as the Turk fastened the star and stepped back, saluting, smiling, already looking about to collect his guard and so take his departure.

"But—" said George Abercrombie Fox. "But." And, just then, that was all he could say.

"You have my sincerest felicitations, my dear sir. Now you are, along with the great Lord Nelson, members of the same Order of the Crescent. I trust this pleases you."

Please him? All manner of frightful problems scorched into Fox's mind. He, a mere lieutenant, could never go parading around with this great glittering star pinned to his uniform coat. He'd pawned the silver medal for the Nile, pawned it immediately he could. That silver medal had not been issued by the Lords Commissioners for the Admiralty, not by a long chalk. Nelson's own agent, his old friend Alexander Davison, it was who had struck the medals in gratitude for being appointed sole agent for the prizes. Gold for the captains, silver for the lieutenants, gilt metal for the petty officers, copper for the seamen and marines. Two thousand pounds, near enough, that gesture had cost Davison. Fox couldn't begin to estimate what this star had cost.

If it was genuine.

His hand went automatically to the star as it gleamed and flashed upon his breast, and Murad saw that gesture, and read the evil look that crossed Fox's face.

He shook his head.

"I should tell you now, Lieutenant. The diamonds are not real." He made a typical Oriental gesture of negation of responsibility. "But you dare not question this. I did not purloin the stones, for my wealth is such that a bauble like this in monetary value is nothing. Who has changed the diamonds for glass? Perhaps the Grand Signor—but, I talk like a man who wishes to feel the garrott. There is nothing you can do. Accept the gift for what it means."

"What it means! If the diamonds are glass it's worth nothing! I could have—I could have—"

Murad had collected his people about him now. He was a powerful man, with great wealth; but he could understand a poor man's despair at seeing riches snatched from his greedy grasp.

"You would have sold—no—what is it—"

"Pawned it!" yelled Fox. "A useless chunk of glass!"

"Think of the good wishes of both Yassin Soliman and Chorbaji Mustafa Murad, who besought this gift for you from the Grand Signor himself. Do you believe you should be rewarded for what you did in the same fashion as Lord Nelson, for what he has done?"

There it was. There lay the enormous gulf between those with fortune and fame and Interest, and those who had none of those delightful perquisites.

The Sultan of Turkey was just as powerful and just as indifferent as any other ruler. He had done according to his lights. Fox should give thanks that he had received even this trinket, for the glittery glass bauble represented much more than it was in itself.

The Turks left *Hector* and Fox stood to see them go. Again he felt the star blazing on his breast. Strange. Strange! A decoration that put him into the same Order as Nelson—and there was no one else of whom he knew

23

in that Order of the Crescent—and he daren't wear the thing. He wondered what old Jarvie would say if he caught sight of a lowly lieutenant parading around with a blazing foreign decoration. There had been enough trouble with Sir Sidney Smith and his Order of the Sword of Sweden, and serving officers called him The Swedish Knight in terms of scorn and derision.

That hauled Foxey up all standing.

A knight!

He hadn't thought—no—impossible!

Surely had there been any intention that he should be known as Sir George Fox—my God! How the name rolled out!—then this Murad acting as an ambassador from the Grand Signor would have told him. Anyway, Fox had the gravest doubts that any damned heathen Sultan had any powers to convey a knighthood, which was as Christian an honor as any. No. No, clearly, any ideas of that sort were impossible.

They might have sent him a bag of gold, just to sweeten the empty gift of the star.

He fingered it again. The dammed thing was decidedly, uncompromisingly, attractive. He knew he would look well wearing the star. He would have to unfasten it—now!—before anyone saw him and rumors flew.

For G. A. Fox honors were unknown quantities. Fighting so desperately for success and to make a living, he had scarcely ever really believed that honors would come his way; as indeed they had not. Yet, yet . . .

He delayed in unfastening, and delayed yet again, and Captain Percy Staunton came out onto the empty quarterdeck, and harrumphed in that foolish traditional naval way, and Fox turned, his hand still upon the glitter of the star.

To his surprise, Staunton did not appear to notice.

Then Fox saw Staunton's face, as long as a fiddle and yet with a strange nervous excitement about it, and a tic beside his mouth that threatened to become either a laugh or a sob.

Now what had happened?

"Mr. Fox—"

Staunton put a hand to his face. That hand clutched a lawn kerchief, white and starched and brilliant.

"Mr. Fox. I have just received the most distressing news."

In the prescribed form, of which when necessary he was a master, Fox said: "I am much concerned to hear it, sir."

"Yes, yes . . . Mr. Fox—you've been as good a damned sea officer as any I've ever sailed with." Staunton let out a laugh that sounded more like a sob, the two were so strongly commingled. "It don't look as though I shall sail again, damme, it surely don't, Mr. Fox."

Fox waited.

Staunton had been reading his letters and the news, Fox saw with a swift and appalled clarity of prediction, held no goods news for him.

"Mr. Fox. I am sorry to tell you that my father, Lord Smithgate, is dead." Before Fox could open his thin mouth to make the prescribed answer, Staunton went on. "And, d'you see, Mr. Fox, William, my eldest brother, and Archie, the next—they were with father when—when the boat sank. They were all drowned."

"Good God!" said Fox, stung from his usual indifference to other people's misery. "I am most distressed, sir, most distressed."

"Thank you, Mr. Fox." Staunton lifted his head to look at Fox. "You're a hard man, Mr. Fox. Damned hard. But —but I shall miss you."

25

If panic ever clawed at G. A. Fox, panic gibbered and clawed at him now.

On the instant, that hateful purple and black ring began to form around his left eye. A relic of an old and forgotten wound, that diabolical pink and black obscuration of his vision attacked him in moments of stress and passion and, as always, he experienced a surge of anger at this crippling of his powers.

"D'you see, Mr. Fox? As the younger son I never thought—never entered my head—just an honorable—and now, damme, here I am Lord Smithgate, Earl of Brinkhampton."

"My congratulations, sir."

Fox would adhere to the good old Navy custom, and treat any titled Lord as just another officer, and Captain or Mister him as he would anyone else. Unless, that was, like that black bastard Beckworth, the fool insisted on being called by his title. Lord Lymm. He had been a real right swine, a man for whom Fox could hold only contempt—and yet, he was realist enough to know that he ought, for the good of his own skin, to tinge that contempt with fear and obedience. For our Percy, now so amazingly a peer of the realm, could Fox harbor similar sentiments?

"I shall have to go ashore at once and post home. There will be a deuced lot to do. And, for all his faults, I was fond of the old feller. He wanted me to be an admiral, and, devil take it, Mr. Fox, you know I ain't a sailor! Now tell me, ain't that the truth on't?"

"You have done very well. Don't forget you were the flag captain of the ship that led four English liners into a victorious action against seven—"

"Now, Goddammit, Mr. Fox! I know who did that!"

Fox was not going to reply. The shoal waters around these emotions contained fanged rocks of destruction.

26

"My uncle Admiral Staunton will be relieved of looking out for me, Mr. Fox. And I've a hankering for a little huntin' and fishin'. I've seen too much salt water."

A strange thought struck Fox, and yet not at all strange, really. Staunton's name would remain on the Captain's List. As the years passed and captains died his name would rise up the List. One day, if he lived, even if he never set foot in a British warship again, Percy Staunton would become an admiral.

Staunton was staring at Fox's uniform coat.

"What the devil is *that*, Mr. Fox?"

Fox told him. He made it brief; but he told Percy Staunton, Lord Smithgate, the Earl of Brinkhampton, and our Percy gawped, and, for a few moments, forgot his own sorrow at the death of his father and brothers, and his succession to a peerage. "I wish you joy of it, Mr. Fox, my oath on't! But, lay me horizontal, you can never wear the confounded thing!"

"I know, sir."

Then Staunton became caught up in the whirl of what he must do and, so quickly it seemed to Fox as though mere moments passed, Staunton was over the side and the quarterdeck once more contained only George Abercrombie Fox.

Strange, strange . . . This morning held doings that were not likely to be repeated. The receipt of a decoration of an Order on the quarterdeck of a stripped and mastless ship; a peerage descending from the clouds, and, worst blow of all, all hope of Staunton's Interest gone. There was no one else, not even Cloughton, in the Navy who would take Interest in Fox.

As usual, he was out on his own, in the cold, from the gutter where he was born looking hopelessly out upon the glitter of a world he was debarred from entering.

27

CHAPTER THREE

There were many letters to be written and appointments
to be kept. Fox had to go on living his life as a naval
officer and make the attempt to secure employment. He
fancied that this should not prove as difficult as it had
done in the past, for now he was known as the first lieutenant of the ship in which Admiral Cloughton had secured so notable if minor a victory. Victory was expected.
Defeat would not be tolerated. The British seaman had
now reached a mood in which miracles were common-
place to him and he would dare any dangers and any odds
and completely fail to understand he might not succeed.
So that Cloughton's Action did not make the kind of stir
such an action would have done only a few years ago.

It was necessary to go up to the tavern and there sniff
the wind and find out what news there was. The papers
must be consulted. He could no longer live aboad *Hector*,
in fact he had at last been paid off, and so Fox took tem-
porary lodgings in a thin-walled and draughty garret
above a chandler's shop. He lived frugally. He could not

make up his mind to return home just yet, for he sensed that here would be the place where opportunity would strike.

He was walking on the Hard one bright morning, fretting as usual, when H.M.S. *Clorinde* sailed in.

On his next visit to the tavern, where he would take his usual abstemious gill of rum, he was not at all surprised to see Lieutenant Lionel Grey.

Fox hesitated on the threshold.

How to meet Grey again? The youngster had done him a great service in bringing him the information that Percy Staunton wanted him as his first, and was creating troubles at home. Well, all those troubles had been laid to rest and those particular routes to fame and fortune had closed.

"Mr. Fox! Durned good to see you again!" And Grey advanced upon him this time openly beaming, his hand outstretched. "Pray allow me, sir, to congratulate you most warmly on your glorious action! It has been the talk of *Clorinde's* gunroom! Why, sir, to outmaneuver and thrash seven o' the line! Magnificent!"

"Thank you, Mr. Grey," said Fox, in his grey and neutral voice. Bigod! Young Grey had changed from that imp of Satan who'd served as a snotty-nosed middy in *Racoon!*

"Magnificent, Mr. Fox. Absolutely splendid. How I cursed I did not have the pleasure and privilege of being with you in the action—"

"Now then, Mr. Grey. I was the first lieutenant. You seem to forget it was Admiral Cloughton, and Captain Staunton—"

Grey looked at him in a most puzzling way.

"Why, of course! But I know—Captain Staunton—and Admiral Cloughton come to that—why, Mr. Fox, devil take it I know how it must have been!"

29

Fox moved closer and interposed his squat and chunky body between the elegant and beautiful uniformed body of Grey and the taproom door. "Maybe you do know how it was, Mr. Grey, and maybe you're dreaming. But I don't think Admiral Cloughton—for one—would wish to be reminded of what might or might not have happened." Now, just how much did Grey know as distinct from what he surmised from his knowledge of Fox? And, how much of that information was common knowledge in the fleet?

"I hold no grudge against Cloughton, Mr. Grey."

That was not strictly true, for nothing had been heard from Cloughton. But with that strange thrilling intimation that great things lay over the horizon, Fox still half-believed his promotion must come through on the morrow as each day succeeded the one before.

And as each day brought nothing so that promise dwindled.

Grey moved a hand dismissingly. "*Clorinde* is doing without me for a space, Mr. Fox. Now, may I have the pleasure of ordering you a brandy, sir?"

Fox wouldn't say no to that.

They turned the conversation onto *Clorinde*'s cruise in which, to Grey's great and openly expressed disgust, nothing had happened. "Only powder we expended was in practice, devil take it. Johnny Crapaud kept his tail well between his legs."

They discussed the topics of the day—the rumors were thicker still of a rift between Saint Vincent and Nelson over the apportionment of the prize money taken by the four British frigates from the Spanish flota. Fox had missed his chance of dipping his arms elbow deep into that silver. The political situation and the Union came under scrutiny. The war was satisfactorily won a dozen time by as many marvellous and foolproof schemes, and Fox woke up to the fact that he and Grey were rapidly going half-seas under.

He stretched out his legs and leaned back on the settle in the window and pointed out the indubitable fact to Grey.

"'pon my soul, Mr. Fox! Dash it, sir, you are right! I think a turn or two might inprove our digestions."

So, companionably, they rolled out onto the street, blinking owlishly in the sunlight.

Just how it all happened, Fox was not too clear; but when he bid Lieutenant Lionel Grey goodbye and staggered off to his garret he was engaged to travel with Grey to Tunbridge Wells on his way home. It would be no diversion. Anyway, Grey was spending some small part of the summer season there with friends, and Fox, he said with great enthusiasm, would find them a perfectly top-hole set of ruffians.

Since Beau Nash with his experiences of Master of the Ceremonies at Bath had taken on the Wells, the Kent watering place had grown in stature and favor. Nash was dead now, of course; and Derrick, also, had gone. But Tunbridge Wells was second only to Bath as a spa of fashion—and many people, because of its proximity to London, preferred it over the Somerset spa. A fast fly could wheel you from the Wells to the capital in five hours or five and a half in bad times. Certainly, Tunbridge Wells queened it over such lesser spas as Scarborough, or Buxton, and Epsome was not to be tolerated by persons of quality. Fox almost opted at once for Epsome, at that.

There were many memories of Lionel Grey in Fox's mind's eys.

He remembered backing the topsail to bring *Raccoon* back to fish Grey out of the drink when they were being chased by a French frigate; they'd fought at Acre together, and Grey had come looking for him at dead of night with a great blunderbuss in his hands, when Fox had escaped from that erotic Turkish harem. They'd caroused together in Gibraltar, when Grey had had to go. Oh, yes, they'd been through a lot together, and the impeccable, amused, elegant Grey with his delighted toleration of this hulking great tarpaulin lieutenant meant more to Fox than he would admit to anyone, and never to himself.

"If Mr. Carker was here now, now," said Grey, and put into words exactly what Fox was thinking. "I do believe we'd enjoy ourselves more than all the lords of the kingdom put together."

Fox whilst never being unaware of that amused regard of him that Grey adopted, had the idea that Grey was trying to civilize him. He'd been officious, Fox remembered, over tha matter of a hat.

On their way into Tunbridge Wells they were beset by crowds of touters screeching the values of their various masters' wares. The Water Dippers, the grocers, butchers, bakers, the tavern keepers, all had their touters out to make a first impression. So suddenly were Grey and Fox set upon that a man of lesser nerve might easily have struck the importuning people down, or shot one of them before the truth was made known.

"Do you ignore them, my dear sirs," exclaimed the stout party in the shawl and the dress that had the greatest difficulty in swathing her portly form. The coach rocked as they moved off. "The wretches cry every year, and every year the story is the same."

"Egad, they make the most infernal hullabaloo," said Grey, laughing, and settling back into his seat.

Fox decided that no amount of screeching would part him from a single penny. He knew about the various subscriptions it would be necessary to pay to enter the

Rooms, and the balls, and even the Taverns and the Bookshop. Varying according to rank, the subscriptions, he was confident, would be on the lowest scale for him. Where he would pay a half crown, Percy Staunton would have to pay a whole guinea.

The Tunbridge Wells bells rang for the new arrivals, and the music played, and, all in all, a very merry time seemed to lie in store. Grey's friends had found a decent lodging for them on Mount Ephraim, which was reckoned to be the finest of the three Mounts on which the lodging houses lay scattered about haphazardly, and Fox felt he wouldn't be able to support this expense for very long. But he was in a peculiar frame of mind. He felt still convinced that Cloughton's letter to the Admiralty must bear fruit. The Gazette had carried the letter. It was bound to do that, for Cloughton's Action, even now and even in the circumstances when absolute victory was the norm, still carried weight. Any day now, any day now—and it would be Commander Fox.

The Pantiles charmed Fox.

He had expected a place of offensive snobbery, of cracked paving tiles pretending to be a walk, of dirty hovels passing themselves off as houses, of draughty barns pretending to be assembly rooms. The reality proved delightful. Tunbridge Wells, surely, was a place—it was scarcely a town—where a man might taste of the good things of life. Always, that was, provided he did not taste the waters which had brought the little spot into being, stealing a name from nearby Tunbridge and adding Wells. The water tasted vile, even to a man who had lived on ship's water.

They dived into the reckless jollity of the proceedings, gambling, wenching, playing, riding donkeys, generally acting as though England was not at war with a mad Cor-

33

sican stirring up a powerful nation to destroy all that was English.

Fox considered himself a card player. That he was also a gambler could not be denied. With friends, with people he felt to be his equals, and with his subordinates, he would play absolutely fairly, and if he won then it was because he was a superb player. With scions of the nobility, who sweated cheap labor, who ground down their workers, who wasted the wealth they had acquired from ancestors who had stolen it in the first place, he was ruthless.

G. A. Fox could play a hand of cards and win when he had to, and if the necessity was great enough and his opponents pressing enough, well, he'd cheat 'em and be damned to 'em. As of now, in this pleasant exploratory period, he played fairly, and won; not a lot, it is true; but enough to sustain his modest daily wants and to make him believe he might keep on with Grey in the Mount Ephraim lodgings ruinous though they were. He had sent money to his family, and was assured they did not want.

Fox was a man of his times. For all that he could not be brought to hate the French, as those in authority assured him every true Briton should. He had had too many experiences in France, in good times and in bad, to make him hate a Frenchman merely because he was a Frenchman. When he got into action, and it was his life or theirs —why, then, the picture changed.

Because of this he could not fail to be aware of the massive weight of authority, where nobility and rank counted for everything. People might talk to whom they pleased when they promenaded the Walks; that was allowed. But the barriers of class went up with a clang like the damned clang of those hideous cell bars in Port Mahon. He was never likely to be invited to the private dinner and gambling parties of the nobs and their ladies. As

34

it was, he got along famously with Grey's circle. They were mainly serving officers, a few bright sparks, dandies, a couple of pinchbeck dandies, also—for whom Fox could not share the general contempt, knowing them brethren under the skin apart from their fawning servility.

He overcame one obstacle very early on.

Grey was used to Mr. Fox bellowing and bawling on the quarterdeck, lashing the hands on to superhuman efforts. Grey might not take kindly to Fox's use of his cutglass voice.

Fox's enormously powerful and retentive memory had served him well in the past, giving him total recall whenever he wished, and providing him with his command of languages. It had also delivered into his hands the means of exactly duplicating in mimicry the speech patterns and accents of other dialects and accents—he had once scared the living daylights out of a mess back in the old *Hermione*, bawling out in the boatswain's voice for them to tumble out. Now, he put on his high-class accent when talking to people of similar station, letting it slide gradually into Grey's consciousness.

Grey had the courtesy not to mention the subject.

He did say: "You will be wearing uniform, Mr. Fox?"

"I don't have any other clothes with me—"

"The tailors here ain't the same as in Town; but, devil take it, Mr. Fox!" and Grey simmered himself down from whatever enormity he had been about to utter.

Fox could sympathize with Grey—and that was an unusual attribute for G. A. Fox to allow himself—and so he said: "A uniform's a very becoming attire, so I'm told, Mr. Grey."

"There are uniforms and uniforms."

"There's a war on. A man should be proud to wear the

35

King's uniform. Aye, and a wench proud to hang on his arm."

Grey favored Fox with that mocking, quizzical glance of his that could so infuriate G. A. Fox if he allowed it to.

Fox guessed Grey knew as well as he did himself that the pompous words and florid sentiments were mere disguises, a smokescreen thrown up to evade the central issue; but no man would find a fault with them. Bigod! There was a war on, and Fox was playing no part in it. Well, the letter for which he craved must come soon from the Admiralty. It must!

And he had neatly side-stepped Grey's probing on the subject of his wardrobe.

All the quality and fashion would come to Tunbridge Wells during the summer season, more, in truth, than would venture to Bath for the winter season there. An amusing thought struck George Abercrombie as he watched the lords and ladies, the dandies, the beaus, all that glittery panoply of English high society as it strutted and promenaded the Walks. He wondered how they would react if this dashing naval lieutenant, whose name had recently appeared in the gazette in Admiral Cloughton's letter in such favorable terms, revealed to them that he had recently taken a horse and barker and a black mask and gone for a highwayman on the high pad. He had not done it for the money—although he would, bigod, he would!—but to punish Lord Rowe. The gang of highwaymen led by William Cogden had dubbed Fox 'Redeye'. They'd held up Lord Rowe's coach—and then Fox left off thinking of highwaymen and thought instead of the gorgeous red-haired green-eyed girl he'd rescued from Rowley Rowe.

She had been a luscious wench, a real tearer, more of a tomboy than not, and yet all woman . . . How, Fox

36

wondered with that peculiar little mental gesture of despair, how was it that whenever he thought of women always in the end his thoughts came around to poor silly fat Sophy, daughter of Lord Kintlesham? Sophy and her father had let him down badly, disastrously, in the Mediterranean, and the silly fat simpering girl who had fancied she was so desperately in love with Fox and gone off with Lord Fotherby, that cowardly adventurer. Poor silly fat Sophy? Yes, he felt sorry for her, that must be it—and then the incongruousness of that struck him, and he went a-roaring off with Grey's cronies into a mad gambling spree.

By circumspection—which was not easy—Fox avoided uncomfortable encounters with the snobs over his lowly parentage. He recalled the story with great affection of how Beau Nash had handled the same problem. Mind you, Nash was recognized as the King of Bath, and also of Tunbridge Wells, and so could take a license denied to a humble naval lieutenant without connections. That autocratic lady the Duchess of Marlborough had taunted Nash on his humble origins, saying of him, like Gil Blas, he was ashamed of his father. Nash had replied marvellously—or so Fox considered.

"No, Madam," Nash had said. "I seldom mention my father in company, not because I have any reason to be ashamed of him, but because he has some reason to be ashamed of me."

That should have put the unpleasant woman in her place.

Fox met similar unpleasant people; but with Grey's charming smile at his ear and Grey's firm grip upon his elbow, he weathered the storms and the shoals. He fought only three duels, minor affairs, and soon the word got around that this Lieutenant Fox was a man not to be trifled with. Fox hated it all and, at last coming to his senses, realized that he was frittering away his time and energies, even if he was making money.

"I'm going home, Mr. Grey. And neither you nor the devil will stop me."

Grey did not look disappointed.

"I am distressed, Mr. Fox," he said. "But, lay me horizontal, sir, you are right. I need a ship."

"Amen to that."

"Tunbridge Wells is the most delightful of spots. But there is a war on, and these people do not care. England could be overrun—even though they see the volunteers—"

"They go out play-acting with the Fencibles. But that is not war as I know it."

"Do you remember when we cap-a-barred a battery of artillery from Boney—?"

"I'm scarcely likely to forget it."

"And the limber, blown up by a single shot—"

"Two nine-pounders were discharged, Mr. Grey."

"Oh, surely. But it was a single shot, all the same."

They strolled gently along the Pantiles, occasionally stopping to look into a window or to exchange a greeting with an acquaintance, and Captain Bolt—whom everyone called Lightning—made sure they bowed correctly whenever the quality passed. This Bolt with his scarlet uniform and scarlet face and scarlet-edged eyes remained a figure of fun to Fox; but for the sake of Grey he suffered the lobster.

Everyone did everything at the same time at the Wells, and to Fox this smacked too much of a daily routine which could become too hidebound; but it was damnably difficult to get anyone—even Grey—to break the conventions and not go to Chapel when so ordained, or to one of the tea shops, Morley's or Upton's, for example, or to listen to the music when it played its three times a day daily ration. He and Grey with Bolt and their cronies as befitted the customs of the place curtailed their dancing or playing in the Rooms at eleven. Most people might then turn in, for lodgings were meant merely for sleeping in, people living in public in Tunbridge Wells. But Bolt had sniffed out a gregarious band of like-minded spirits, and in a certain house Fox and Grey and the others might play long into the night with the candles burning down and their glasses religiously topped up.

On their last evening, at cards, Fox and Grey made the most of it. On the morrow Grey was off home, and Fox was going to the narrow wooden house by the Thames. After that they made a compact to travel to the Admiralty and there see what employment could be found for them.

The lamplight gleamed mellowly on the shoulders of the women, on the evening clothes of the men, winked from silver candelabra, sheened from the playing cards. Fox was winning comfortably, fairly, and Grey, at another table, was losing badly. Fox caught his look of annoyance and suspicion as he glanced over at Fox. Later, with a casual skill, Fox changed tables. He sat down with all his nervous energy tensed up and controlled, so that he moved with the languid elegance so much admired. "You appear to be on a lee shore with not a hook left, Mr. Grey."

"The devil take it, Mr. Fox! My timbers are taking water faster than the pumps can remove it."

Fox watched the play carefully. He was a remarkably good player; also he could card-sharp with the best. He very soon had the cheat spotted. He looked at the fellow. Stout, bald-headed, with pinched lines at each side of his nose, the man yet had a great generous mouth that laughed a very great deal and his eyes twinkled right mer-

39

rily as his supple fingers stacked the cards with dexterity. His plain clothes were models of good taste. He was, one could see at a glance, a pillar of respectability. His winnings proclaimed he was also either a good player or lucky. He could not be a cheat, could he, not here, not in sacred Tunbridge Wells?

Fox went to work on him.

The man's pinched nose pinched deeper. His generous mouth lost all its merry laughter. His eyes went piggy mean.

When etiquette allowed conversation Fox made polite meaningless remarks. Grey's winnings mounted. Grey stared rather too hard at Fox. At last Fox felt Grey had recompensed himself sufficiently, and when it was convenient to do so he rose, forcing himself to smile upon the little group who had collected. It was half past ten and almost time for them all to retire.

Grey rose also, and they stood for a moment as the others shuffled into new arrangements, candlelight gleaming, fans fluttering, the cards being collected up.

"A strange business, Mr. Fox, Deuced strange."

"You should, Mr. Grey, stand off a lee shore. You were seen safely through your examination for lieutenant, as I know—you and Mr. Carker both—and that is the question they ask." Fox turned to go. "The fellow was a mere cheat."

"But," said Grey, and Fox cursed his great waggling tongue.

Oddly, Grey had not gone on, and Fox heard him draw in his breath, as though something had dug him below the ribs.

"My God!" Grey whispered. "What a beauty!"

This was a hunting call. Fox turned swiftly. The girl who had walked past, impeccably gowned, gorgeous, lithe

40

in the long clinging skirts of her dress, a bare blaze of flesh above the low neckline, had red hair and green eyes.

She saw Fox.

"Why!" she exclaimed. "This is a surprise and a pleasure! How are you, Mr. Redeye?"

CHAPTER FOUR

Being Lieutenant Fox came sometimes as a sore trial to George Abercrombie Fox. And, equally, being G. A. Fox with all that meant, sometimes became an insupportable monolith to Mr. Fox.

At the moment, with early morning sunshine streaming in past the half-closed curtains and falling in rods of radiance across the tumbled bed, with the debris of last night's return to his lodgings scattered about the room, a shoe here, a stocking there, his coat crumpled on the floor somewhere near the stand at which he aimed it, his shirt caught up with the other shoe and trailing from a bedpost, a chemise petticoat and a white gown tangled up with the rest, the candle all bent and squashed where'd he'd bashed it out . . . A chemise? A white gown?

About to sit up with something of uncomprehending horror upon him, Fox felt a long naked white arm flop over his equally naked chest. He looked sideways in the bed. A spreading mass of red hair stained the pillow in the raidance piercing past the curtain. He saw a white rounded shoulder, and deep blue shadows, and the arm moved again, slender fingers opening and closing gently, and Miss Jennie Blane sighed and said: "You are a devil, George."

"Amen to that," he groaned.

After a time, when activity ceased to roil the bed clothes, Fox looked at Jennie Blane and tried to put a most serious expression on his face, and succeeded only in making her laugh at him.

"Oh, George!"

"The question is, Jennie, what is to be done with you?"

"Well—I cannot go out dressed like this at this time in the morning—"

"All the ladies go in deshabille first thing—"

"I know. But that undress is just as much a dress as anything else we wear during the day."

"Then I shall have to smuggle you back to your lodgings."

Jennie Blane had not only completely forgiven Fox for his mad adventure as Redeye the highwayman, she was particularly grateful. Fox had pulled one-eyed Walsh off her. He had also bought back the golden locket stolen from between her naked breasts by William Cogden. In returning the locket he had attempted some explanation. She had shushed him.

"I knew at once you were not a highwayman, George. Had it not been for you—" And here she shivered and all the joy faded. She remembered with a very terrible terror her encounter with Lord Rowe, whom men called Rowley Rowe. "And my cousin, Jack,—and—well—it was awful."

"Hush, Jennie."

"We are not a wealthy family; but afterwards Jack

43

didn't care a fig for his money that Gentleman Jack stole. We had to nurse that beast Lord Rowe all the way."

"I'm afraid there was no chance of regaining your cousin Jack's money, for all that he is a sea officer."

"But I'm wickedly glad they robbed Rowley Rowe! The man is a beast."

Fox did not enlighten Jennie Blane as to his reasons for being mixed up with highwaymen. But he had a shrewd idea she could guess, in view of the thrashing the highwaymen had given the noble lord, that robbery was not the motive.

Now, this morning, after their night's encounter, in which all the tomboyish aspects of Jennie Blane had mingled so electrifyingly with her sensual womanliness, Fox had to get her back to her lodgings. Scandals made up the stuff of life at the Wells. Lampoons were written for the book in the Library, and Fox, having already featured in some execrable rhymes by some unknown who fancied himself a second Pope, had no wish to have his name linked with that of Miss Jennie Blane.

His full dress uniform, the one bought from the loan from Percy Staunton, had sustained some damage during Cloughton's Action, thus causing the offense to Mr Grey's subsceptibilities; but it was still smart. Fox urged Jennie into her underclothes—God knew, they were few enough, girls were wearing practically nothing at all these days—and then dragged the uniform coat over her shoulders. Fox's own stature was sufficient for the coat to hang voluminously on Jennie; but her breasts—superb, considered Fox, stuffing them in their thin material into the uniform—filled out the blue cloth with its white facings. He made no attempt to do the buttons up across the chest as was becoming very much the fashion with the smarter type of naval officer these days. Gentlemen no longe

44

wore swords as a matter of course in public, in fact they were prohibited in the Wells, so that there was no chance of the baldric adding to the deception.

"You're treating me like a barrel of lard, George! God! That's my nipple you've pinched!"

"You know lodgings are not meant to be lived in, Jennie, my turtle dove. Can you get my breeches over your delightful hips? Good—pull, gal, pull! We've to be out of here with the utmost despatch—that is, if you care a fig for your reputation."

"My reputation is above reproach."

"I agree." He gave her rump a slap. "Now the boots—damnation—they're all I have!—and you'll pass—"

"Oh, George!" She flounced onto the bed as Fox pushed her and started levering and hauling and maneuvering the boots over the feet and calves. "This is ridiculous! I don't look like a man—my hair!"

"That is all taken care of."

He got the boots on and then fetched a white towel. This he wrapped around Jennie's hair, and let a long fall drape down one side. He clapped his best hat on the top. He stepped back. "You look extraordinary, I declare. But you must stare with all that damn-you-to-hell look in your eyes if anyone accosts us. You've a fever—yes?"

Jennie Blane was a high spirited gal. She laughed.

"The sun is already hot enough to fry eggs! I shall stifle, I do declare."

"Stifle away, my gal. Come on."

Custon came to their assistance. Custom decreed that everyone should go a-walking on the Walks at this time, early on, before the real business of the day began, and during this time with the ladies in undress assignations were made and contracts for riding or gaming or any of the other petty activities of the ensuing day. Fox and Jennie

45

scampered along between the trees and kept mighty low whenever anyone—who was, of course, no-one—passed by. As there were two Walks in the Wells, the upper and the lower, for respective classes of society, so the wheat-eater sellers and the fruit sellers and all the laboring classes might espy these two odd-looking naval officers— one with a fever bandage massed about his head—but their talk would in their own uncouth fashion remain among themselves. Fox writhed at this idea. But, goddam-mit to hell! Jennie had been kind. He owed her at the least this gesture of gallantry.

The notion of gallantry co-existing with all the other notions seething in G. A. Fox's brain struck him as ludi-crous.

Skirting very wide of the Pump room and the Chapel of Ease and keeping low they gained the house in which Jen-nie lodged.

"I positively cannot go into the front door, George!"

Fox took her hand and drew her around the back, past a screen of shrubbery. He eyed the windows, flashing i the morning sun. He cocked his head. "Which?"

"That one—"

"Of course," said Fox. "The second floor. I might have known."

No ladder presented itself to Fox's gaze. He could have himself shinnied up there in a twinkling; he could manage it with Jennie over his back, he supposed, think-ing of what that kind of treatment would do to his uniform —no, bigod!—to both his uniforms!

His eyes, questing about, fell upon a donkey placidly eating away in the adjoinig field.

All the deviltry that had lain so dormant in George Abercrombie these past months reared up with the most delightfully wicked leer.

He secured the donkey by the rope halter and, with a surprising ease that betokened he might have to urge the beast to activity later, led it around to the side of the house. Jennie followed wonderingly.

"Now, Jennie, I suppose the stairs are inside the hall? Right? Well, then, as soon as the way is clear do you go boldly in and run up the stairs. You've no hampering skirts, and your lower limbs are as fine as anyone's—"

"George!"

"So, Jennie, my luscious armful, when I shout—run!"

With that Fox led the donkey around to the front door. Two maids were there banging brooms and brushes and feather dusters in a great cleaning up after the gentry. The donkey, urged on in no uncertain manner by Fox's foot, hee-hawed and charged for the door, with Fox clinging to the halter and steering him as he might steer a surf boat going in over the West African surf. The maids shrieked and fell every which way. Fox had to hoick up the nearest and send her careering in the door. Her stockinged legs kicked in a froth of white. Her mob cap fell off, spouting pins, and her black hair fell about her face.

"Lawks a'mussy! I'm killed! Help! Help!"

The donkey hee-hawed splendidly.

The two maids gathered themselves together and in a flail of arms and legs and waving hair fled into the back portions of the house.

This did not satisfy G. A. F.

He gave the donkey a most unsubtle kick and the animal, with a magnificent bray, bolted into the open doorway, over the carpet, into the hall. Staggering along with the halter gripped in hands that had held sheets in gales that stripped a ship of her spars and canvas in a twinkling, Fox steered the animal past the stairs and through the far door. A panelled hall led away and in the distance came

47

the sound of pans banging and shrieks and a general pandemonium.

"Go, on, Ned!" said Fox, giving the donkey one last slap. "Go down there and deliver your broadside!"

The donkey careered madly down the passage. Much though he would have liked to see the donkey coming into action, Fox swung back. At the main door he yelled: "Jennie!"

She appeared, a blue and white figure running, and he observed how her tophamper surged with the quickness of her movements. She came up with him. Her face glowed. Fox had no sign of sweat on him.

"You men!" said Jennie Blane. "You don't know how lucky you are not having horrible skirts to impede running!"

"Maybe," said Fox. "But you can't see right through a pair of britches."

"Oh, George! I knew you were no gentleman and I love you for it—but—"

"No time for buts. Get up them stairs!"

She cast him a glance that made Fox spread his thin lips in that horrific grimace that passed as a smile, and she fled.

The noise from the back part of the house was now a most gorgeous cacaphony. It was with great regret that Fox decided discretion was the better part of valour. He firmly intended seeing Miss Jennie Blane again—and again—and to be spotted now for that ugly Lieutenant Fox would ruin all the scheme. He chuckled. He really did. Then he trotted off back to carry on the normal day's activities. Or, at least, those parts of the daily charade he cared to indulge in.

There was no doubt about it. Living in Tunbridge Wells made a man soft in the head. Or, at least, tended to suborn him from the wilder and harder aspects of the life a sailorman knew as normal. Tunbridge Wells was altogether too much fun and frolic and lazy good-living, a life that could suck a man in and make him believe he was the center of God's universe.

As though to prove that and to spit in the eye of the devil, the following days turned out to be filled with the purple and gold of high living for Fox. Grey had taken himself off, as they had agreed, and Fox found himself caught up with the racy crowd of which Captain Lightning Bolt was a scarlet and foremost member.

However much Fox knew he ought to see about the Admiralty and a fresh employment, the clinging and yet openly free love of Jennie Blane held him trapped. He drank more than he should have done, and he played cards and the devil's own luck stayed with him, for, as a naturally expert player, he found he could win handsomely without the need of sharping.

The bald-headed man—he scorned a wig—with the narrow eyes and the generous mouth whom Fox had fleeced on behalf of Mr. Grey continued at the Wells. Fox did not run across his hawse again until an evening in that certain private house where many of the bloods and their ladies congregated after the official festivities closed down at eleven. These were the people who sometimes were seen in Chapel, and sometimes were seen taking the Waters; but when they did so were the butts of much scornful laughter from their friends. Notorious, yes, they were that; but Fox went along with them for the sake of Jennie Blane, to whom they proved the fascination of the snake for the rabbit.

This house had been organized in much the same way as any of the many Rooms that might be found in fashionable spas, or in Town, or in the dockyard ports much frequented by the Navy. One difference was that the games of chance in which the players could give full vent to their emotions as the gambling went on shared the same room with the more scientific card games. With Hazard, whist, vingt-et-un, Basset and Lansquenet, for example, played cheek by jowl, not only were chance and skill paraded together but also lawful and unlawful games. The players were discreet. No one wished for a scandal.

Fox if given the opportunity preferred skill. But, when it came to push of pike, he could sharp with the best at whatever game happened to have caught the fancy of the players. Now he found himself seated with four others, one of whom was Jennie, at a table with this bald-headed, mean-eyed, laughing-mouthed man. He called himself Tobias Anstruther, and, for all that Fox knew to the contrary, that was his name.

The limit had been agreed at ten pounds a card. Notes fluttered to the table—crisp five pound notes and some of these new and already unpleasant one pound notes. Gold seemed to be scarcer all the time, and Fox knew that a trade was growing in meeting incoming ships with a view to buying golden guineas at a shilling or two above their value. He had won enough so that he could sit in this fast company. If thoughts of the old wooden row house by the Thames occurred to him he could comfort himself in the knowledge that he had sent home a sizeable proportion of his winnings.

Now, facing this Tobias Anstruther, he began to lose.

Losing in many areas of life had been endemic with Fox. He did not propose to sit quietly and be cheated at cards. So, with a few of those deft manipulations he had practiced for hour after hour through the long nights at sea, he swung the course of the game. He could feel the thickness of the wad of notes beautifully swelling under his fingers.

Jennie laughed at him. "Faith, Mr. Fox. You have the luck of the devil."

Fox remembered the occasion when that surprising Italian nobleman, Benedetto Fogazzaro, had accused him of cheating, and the meeting by that old grey seminary wall. Well, he'd scraped through that with a fine panache; he was not willing to have stories circulate about him and so must be circumspect. Come to think of it, though, there were stories circulating about Mr. Fox, bawdy stories of brothels used to capture Spanish first rates, and stories of cap-a-barring a battery of Boney's artillery, and now the latest, that he had been first lieutenant of *Hector* in Cloughton's Action.

Fox forced his face into that disastrous grimace.

"I may be a devil, madam; but luck has not generally favored me."

She pouted back at him. She hadn't liked the meanings behind that.

Just to be on the safe side he manipulated some of the cards so that they would turn up to give Jennie a match —matching here in the French sense of winning—and she was as brazen as any in her smiles of triumph as she picked up the notes. Play went on and all Anstruther's cunning failed against Fox's stratagems. He'd played Neapolitans on his birthday in Naples and beaten them; Anstruther was good; Fox was just that much better.

Looking up from the play with the candle-light gleaming he saw a knot of men—big, broad-shouldered men in army and navy uniforms, men in fine clothes of the latest dandy-cut,—clustered about a person to whom, it seemed, they were giving every mite of their attention. Fox caught a glimpse of a long straight back in a white gown, sheer and semi-transparent, and the hint of rounded forms beneath. He could not see the girl's face for the shoulder of a marine who leaned across in his anxiety to be one of the inner group around her. She half-turned to reveal the low line of her dress, the firm upthrust of her breasts and the blue ribbons caught beneath. As she moved he saw the firmness of her thighs pressing against the gown, and he realized that she was a beauty, fully deserving of the homage being paid to her.

"La, Mr. Fox!" declared Jennie, without looking over her shoulder to follow Fox's eyes. "We're waiting!"

Fox turned up the two cards at his left, and one for himself and with his usual clumsy way managed to get the rejouissance card into the middle of the table. Bank notes were placed and Fox began to turn up cards, to the quick and avaricious attention of the punters. He won, as he had intended, and Tobias Anstruther shoved up from the table, his whole face indicative of a great wrath held only just in check. He managed to contrive a polite goodnight for the company and took himself off.

Fox was looking for that divine body he had glimpsed through the press of manly bodies; but the girl and her retinue had left. Shortly thereafter Jennie yawned, and Fox, who had felt himself grow exceeding hot through that single glance, that mere glimpse, of the unknown girl, finished the hand and swept up his winnings and bowed a polite goodnight.

He waited outside, in the warm darkness with the stars high and spread above him. Bigod! How he'd welcome the chance to see those stars gyrating from side to side as a deck beneath him bore up and down over the sea!

Jennie joined him, circumspectly, and they walked in a companionable silence to her lodgings. Fox had worked out that it was a deal easier for him to leave by that window in the early hours than to repeat another escapade with the donkey.

That story had gone the rounds, and lampoons had appeared; thankfully, Jennie's name was not implicated.

He proved once again that Jennie Blane was a gorgeous romp and then he took himself off. He was only marginally tired and he strode between the trees towards his lodgings musing over the happenings of the day, and the money he had won, and Jennie, and that strange girl whose form had so moved him, and what his chances of a ship might be.

Tobias Anstruther and his three cronies were clever and quick. They almost topped George Abercrombie Fox before he was aware. But they did not know that Fox had fought Red Indians as a boy, and was always alert, as befitted a sea officer, and so was able to duck and twist sideways and stick out a hard leg and trip the first ruffian. Fox did not stop to him him as he went down but leaped away from the toppling body and, bending over, ducked the next cudgel and drove forward. He put a fist into the guts of number two. He swivelled and kicked number three. Number four yelled. That was Anstruther. By this time number one was on his feet again, still bent, like a fool, and Fox kicked him in the face. He went over backwards spraying the remnants of bone and gristle and blood from a smashed nose.

Fox jumped for Anstruther.

"You black bastard! Get your cronies on me, would you—"

And Fox struck him—twice. The first time he hit him in the stomach. The second time he brought his knee up so that Anstruther's large and generous mouth squashed bloodily.

Among the shrieks of pain Fox's curses sounded like a wolf's firceness among lambs' bleatings.

He hit them as they tried to stagger up, and when they at last lay like four logs, he kicked them a few times, according to his principles. Mercy, for Fox, was a rare and precious commodity, seldom ever received, and administered with a reciprocal lavishness.

He made sure that Anstruther was still conscious.

"Listen, you whoreson! You are a cheat, a sharp, a thief. And I am not some chicken to be plucked. I'm not some dandy from Town. You try anything more silly, Anstruther, and I'll break your arms off."

He debated serving Anstruther as he had served Puggy, decided enough was enough—for civilization had been working on G. A. Fox—and with a final kick at Anstruther's head, rolled off to his just bed.

CHAPTER FIVE

Twice a week a ball was held and only through Jennie's insistence could Fox be prevailed upon to attend. He went with a bad grace. He could dance, and with the closest attention to what he was doing, so that it became all a matter of concentration. In Naples, now, it had been different . . .

The protocol, the white dresses, the glittering uniforms, the elegant clothes of the civilians, the heat and the candles and the wine and dainty foods, the whole shooting match bored Fox silly. Had he not been forced, by custom, to dance only twice with Jennie, for all her charms, he would have found the whole tiresome affair insupportable. As it was he asked a number of ladies if they would care to dance, all in the prescribed form, in his cut glass voice, as he knew was required, and he did his duty.

He stood out for as many dances as he could. He stood in a quiet corner, beyond the row of gilt settees and chairs where the older women—companions, aunts, chaperones —sat with fluttering fans and nodding heads and incessant gossip. His first two fingers of his left hand idly rubbed back and forth across the tiny stomach bulge that he regarded as an obscenity. He surveyed the company, flushed and gleaming, prancing away under the lights, with the music scraping and fiddling away. He'd paid good money for that music and the damned blagskites just set up a caterwauling. Fox had strict tastes where music was concerned. Apart from sailor's songs, which he'd roar out with the best of 'em, he'd been anxious to hear some of the newer symphonies from the continent, out of Germany somewhere. He wouldn't waste a lot of time on finding out about music, not when there was a pretty wench to tumble; but at moments like this he knew what he knew about music.

A group of men leaving the ball attracted his attention, and then, as though he mordantly repeated his experience at the card table, he saw the gorgeous girl. She walked with a swing and a lithe grace that fascinated Fox. Her elegance, her slimness, made him suck in his cheeks. She was a beauty, and yet he still could not clearly distinguish her face. Her hair reminded him—in a cliché that he found perfectly reasonable because it was true—of summer sunshine gleaming on a field of corn. She held that head erect, high, and as she left he caught, for a fraction of a second, a glimpse of her small rounded chin and the long sweet line of throat. Then she had gone.

He had no wish to ask Jennie.

A soldier, brutally stuffed into his scarlet coat and his face seeming by turns as scarlet as his coat and as white as his breeches, stood close by. To him, Fox addressed his query.

"You may well ask, my dear sir. For that is beauty incomparable, divine! She has slain every heart. For myself, a simple soldier, I could ask no greater share of glory than to die at her feet—"

Fox contained himself. This fellow was no real soldier, being one of the volunteers; and Fox knew what Boney's veterans would do to them; but he had to be humored. He was probably an honorable or something of like kidney. They said that everyone knew everyone at the Wells; but this was not strictly true. People arrived and departed all the time, and the fashion of paying calls upon new arrivals was not followed here.

"She is the Duchess of Bowden—Aphrodite, Helen, Juliette. Adorable, quite, quite adorable . . ."

Fox left the soldier to his broken heart. The group that seemed always to surround the beautiful duchess had left; he felt warm towards Jennie, and he knew she would be nothing loath. At the first opportunity he dragged her away. She came willingly enough. He worked his way around to the unknown beauty, and Jennie gave a delightful pout.

"Trust you, George, to have an eye! She is a mysterious woman, right enough. La, I do declare, she is known as so highly autocratic she scarce deigns to speak to anyone less than a baron. And she is rich, confoundedly rich." Jennie had picked up scathing language from her cousin, Jack Blane, who, being a serving sea officer in His Majesty's Navy, picked it up at its fruity source. "She sits on an estate over at Bowden, that was Beauden until they took King Charles's head off, that makes one faint to think of. They don't call her the Melting Duchess for nothing."

Fox had heard of the Melting Duchess. The references made it plain that the melting referred to other people, their estates, finances and hearts, never to the grand lady herself. She was, considered Fox, just one of those female nobility who demanded to be strung up at the nearest lamp post. Let his brother Archie loose there—and all the committees of public safety in the land wouldn't save that pretty white neck.

All the same, all the same—there had been about her slender form, the elegance of her movements, and that maddening glimpse of her chin and throat, an allurement that set him afire. Bigod! To lust after just one especial woman had always seemed a madness. And to lust after such an one with only a single glimpse in passing by smacked of utter idiocy.

Very firmly, Fox put the Melting Duchess out of his mind. With the body of Jennie blazing in the light of the candle as she stretched out on the bed, waiting for him, that was an easy thing to accomplish.

Jennie made him very happy that night and so he was more tender to her than usual the following day. They spent most of it on an excursion to the High Rocks arranged by Lightning Bolt, and came back by pre-arrangement to a late night party devoted to cards, drinking and any other devilments that might occur to the beaus and sparks and dandies who, with their ladies—of various shades of virtue—made up the gathering.

Except for the occasion when Tobias Anstruther had for the second time to be put down, Fox had not cared to cheat with Jennie around. He played fairly. He won. He drank brandy, and cursed and crowed with the best of them. All the refinements of high living surrounded him. He had fought for these things. Candlelight, the gleam of women's bare shoulders, the filled glasses, with only the best old brandy, the close sensual atmosphere of love and passion intertwining with the other passions as the cards fell. He had fed well. He was relaxed and as happy as, perhaps, outside of home, he would ever be on shore.

Jennie sat at his side, laughing, brilliant, a flame with

her red hair and green eyes in that room where license more and more took control of the gathering.

Lightning Bolt, for one, had removed his scarlet uniform and was sitting in his shirt and breeches, a girl on his lap, laughing and roaring at her sallies. The candlelights lent an aura of romanticism to the scene. On the green baize of the table the cards fell and were turned, the money passed, the punters drew in their breaths, or groaned, or laughed.

Jennie leaned close to Fox, her low neckline slipping lower, her bare shoulders magnificent.

He drank deeply, and roared: "Bigod, Jennie! You're bringing me luck tonight!"

"Egad, Mr. Fox, Mistress Jennie would bring anyone luck!" shouted Sam Hoskins, his neckcloth disarranged, his eyes wild, more than half drunk. He leered on Jennie.

"Play, Goddam you, Sam, play!" said his companion, a tall sallow man whose fingers manipulated the cards with assurance and whose eyes followed their every movement; but whose stock of bank notes passed steadily across to Fox.

A girl laughed shrilly from a sofa by the wall. The brandy bottles were emptied and flung into a corner. The lights shone across the scene. Close, scented, abandoned, the wild party racketted on. The door opened and Fox saw a young lieutenant of the army and a young lieutenant of the navy attempting to allow the other to precede one or t'other into the room. They backed and filled like Thames barges in a foul reach. Fox chuckled at that, scooping up his winnings. He clutched a fistful of notes. Jennie laughed at his side, her green eyes dancing, her dress caught so low all the swell of her breasts visible. She laughed, wildly.

"Bigod, Jennie, my love!" shouted Fox. He was more

than half drunk. "Bigod, Jennie! You've brought me luck!"

Jennie laughed again, swaying, leaning down with the brandy glass in her hand. She bent and kissed Fox full on the lips. He responded lustily. She broke free, laughing, swaying, her red hair a tumbled mass across her bare shoulders.

"Here's to you, George!"

Fox took the proffered brandy and raised the glass to his lips. He looked up.

A girl stood in the doorway, the navy to one side, the army to the other. Other men followed her. She wore a long white gown, sheer and yet rounded with the hint of fresh thighs beneath the thin material. Her slenderness, her elegance, the jewels about her bare arms, the high arrogant thrust of her breasts, all captivated Fox. He remained with the glass to his lips, like a loon.

He looked at her face beneath that corn gold hair.

He saw her blue eyes, the sweetness of her face with its small nose and trembling mouth, the redness of the lips, the pallor of the cheeks. He saw a quick flash of incomprehension on that beautiful face, and then a pain, and then a stony mask of disdain.

For that brief betraying moment Fox did not recognize her.

The scintillating brilliance of her tiara, the massed fire of the gems encircling her slender neck, the jewels on her wrists and fingers, all blazed like cruel and cutting bayonet-points into Fox's bemused eyes. He hiccoughed and the brandy slopped. He was a drunken sot, with a half-naked girl hanging on him, a fistful of money clutched in his other hand.

He looked up—and he saw.

"Sophy!"

She stood for a single instant, unutterably beautiful, slender, slim, elegant—gorgeous and so hot that Fox felt himself catch fire.

He tried to stand up, and staggered, and the brandy glass went smash and a couple of bottles fell to roll and scutter brandy across the table. Men yelled angrily and girls squealed. He tried to stand up, and Jennie was clasping him and the room was spinning in heat and stifling closeness in the candlelights.

"*Sophy!*"

She turned. Without a word she turned her elegant back on him and walked from the room. Her steps were smooth and she walked like a goddess, and Fox was left like a red-faced drunken boor, staring after her.

That—*that* was Sophy, poor silly fat Sophy, the daughter of Lord Kintlesham.

Where had all the fat gone? Where the red-splotched thick arms? Where the massive scarlet cheeks? Where the hair that fell everywhere about her in an untidy mess? Where had the roll of fat around her stomach gone? Fox knew. Fox knew. She had grown up. She had lost her puppy fat. She had ceased being a funny fat little girl and had metamorphosed into this stunningly beautiful woman.

He slumped back into his seat.

She no longer looked thirty-five or forty, raddled and red and fat. She looked elegant and cool and gorgeous and she now looked her real age, which must be little short of twenty-three or four.

Fox thought then of Lord Fotherby—and he swore so vilely that even Jennie backed away.

"George! What is it, George! Are you ill?"

"No, Jennie—" He forced himself to remain sane. "No Jennie. Just my sinful past catching up with me." What was one woman to George Abercrombie Fox? Didn't he tumble every lovely lass he could? Well, then? What of Kitty Huggins, and Rosaria, Mildred, what of Angela the Bitch?

So why was Sophy any more than any of them?

He plunged recklessly into play, and still he won; and no one there could hold him. All could see he didn't care for the fall of the cards, and plunged wildly; but still he won.

Later he was able to gather more from Captain Bolt, as Lightning shrugged on scarlet uniform, bleary-eyed, tired.

"Yes, she was married to Lord Fotherby, Mr. Fox. It is a strange story. Lord Fotherby was run down by a runaway horse and cart as they stepped from the church on the wedding day—"

Jennie had gone to ready herself for the return to her lodgings. Fox listened with distaste and yet with a fascination he could not control.

"The story becomes stranger, Mr. Fox. She waited some time and there was a rumor that she wished to accompany her father Lord Kintlesham to Palmero; but the political situation with Boney and all—well, in fine, she married the old Duke, the Duke of Bowden." Here Lightning Bolt laughed, a silly, giggling, drunken laugh. "Bowden was very very rich and very very old. No one knows for sure, of course; but . . ."

The rumors were rife, ripe and scandalous. The facts were that on the morning after the wedding day the servants had been called and there lay the Duke of Bowden, in his huge old bed with his nightcap half-over his face, as dead as a doornail. Sophy had been beautiful, by all accounts, even then, and had become more beautiful with every passing day. Just how the old Duke died, no one knew; but the tale went that Sophy was still a virgin, and the poor old feller had died out of sheer excitement.

"And, d'you see, Mr. Fox. She's a virgin still, and filthy

62

rich, and so beautiful it knocks a man's eyes out—and so all the eligible young men are agog to wed her." Lightning Bolt laughed his foolish laugh again. "They all don't give a damn about the dangers. They're queueing up to see if it will be third time lucky."

Fox understood now. The beaus would be afire to take their chances, gamble that they would be the third time lucky for poor silly fat Sophy—no, bigod! Poor silly fat Sophy had gone for ever. Now she was gorgeous, wonderful, elegant, sheerly womanly Sophy.

Bigod!

It didn't bear thinking of.

He was glad to hear Fotherby had been run over by a horse and cart. He didn't give a damn about the old Duke whose lusts had overpowered his heart.

Jennie was anxious to leave. Fox just could not bring himself up to the mark, not in his present frame of mind.

This astonished Jennie.

She was sharp with G. A. Fox.

"Don't tell me you've been smitten by the Melting Duchess, George!"

"Hardly likely, my girl."

"She's a bitch. She don't care for anyone, not man nor woman, either. I tell you, George, she and Lord Rowe would make a fine match."

Sheer horror, the panic of hell, clutched Fox's guts.

That could not be allowed. Heaven, for which Fox had a healthy regard in times of trouble, would not let that blasphemy be, surely?

Stunned, he allowed Jennie to lead him along, her hand firmly tucked under his own and guiding him. In the end she had her way with him, and he groaned and rolled about and all the time he saw that white blaze of glory that was Sophy, her grace the Duchess of Bowden, dancing tanta-

lizingly before him, mocking, demanding, rejecting, spurn-
ing.

One thing he told himself for sure as he turned into his
own bed, one thing was absolutely clear. He was not in
love with Sophy. He couldn't allow that. Had he the
chance to marry her now, as he had once had when she
was fat and pathetic, he would still marry her, for the
same reasons as had impelled him then. She represented
Interest. With Interest he could secure a posting, gain a
ship, get prize money, perks, make a decent living—and
all this he did so that his family of Foxes by the Thames
should not starve.

CHAPTER SIX

The jolly boat bucked in a cross sea and stroke's oar skittered across the water, decapitating a wave-top and flinging it straight into Fox's face. Fox blinked. He did not curse. He heard the coxswain mutter something, and the jolly boat corkscrewed for a moment; then she came under control again. Stroke bent to his oar and Fox could think in a warm benign fashion of the horrors the seaman must be contemplating.

As for George Abercrombie Fox, nothing could disturb his good temper. Absolutely nothing. Why, the jolly boat might fill and founder for all he cared. He'd simply swim the distance to his brig and clamber aboard, grinning like a loon.

Oh, yes.

He'd go aboard his brig very happily in any condition.

His brig.

His brig.

His Britannic Majesty's Shop *Minion* might be a ghastly sailing vessel, incredibly wet and unseaworthy,

massively armed with sixteen thirty-two pounder carronades—Fox licked his lips at the thought of letting that little lot off in a sequence of almighty bangs—and two six
pounders, with accommodation no self-respecting highwayman would care to inhabit on the night before he kept
his appointment at Tyburn Tree, and was able to claw
into the wind with the same power as a floating saucer,
she was all this, and worse—but, she was *his*.

His—*Minion* was the command of Commander Fox.

On that very next morning after his disastrous re-en-
counter with Sophy, Fox had packed up to leave Tunbridge Wells. There had been nothing of making up his
mind, the decision to leave simply happened. The Post
came in early, as it happened that day, just before eleven.
There was a letter from Admiral Cloughton. Fox had had
to read it twice before its import sank in.

Cloughton wrote, he said, to be the first to give him the
no doubt welcome news that he was to be promoted Commander. He would see the announcement in the *Gazette*.
A ship had been found—and here Fox sensed wheels
within wheels, and the hand of Percy Staunton and of his
puissant uncle, Admiral Staunton—and his letter that
would form his order for taking command would follow.
When Fox had broken the black seal with the Admiralty
impression firmly stamped into the wax,—no wafer for so
weighty a matter as this—he had felt surprise that his
hands had not trembled. He had never believed in the
power of emotions to conquer the bodily functions, unless
you took that damned left eyeball of his into account, and
yet, the emotions with which he read that he was hereby
required and directed to proceed on board *Minion* and
there take upon himself the Charge and Command of the
vessel—and all the rest of the lovely words that rolled and
echoed around his skull—forced him into silent parox-

ysms of glee and joy and sheer outright convulsions of glory. Even those ominous and chilling words: 'Hereof nor you nor any of ye may fail as you will answer the contrary at your peril' could not pierce the golden glow that encompassed him.

He found he kept on feeling his thin lips ricking back in his ghastly parody of a smile. He was like a grinning idiot. He rubbed his hands together. His Commission had already been read aboard, the assistant-master, Watson, had seen to that in all the due ceremony and panoply that tradition required. And how sweet it was to step aboard to the sound of the boatswain's call! Incredible. Sergeant Dunn and his marines paraded for his honor, and presented arms with their loud mechanical clicking and clacking that sounded like the most divine music, better by far than all those Germanic symphonies he had been talking of in Tunbridge Wells.

He had commanded before, notably *Raccoon*; now he was a *real* Captain—or, at the least, a Commander, called captain,—of his very own ship—or, rather, sloop.

Mind you, stroke, a tough whiskery man with a broken nose called Hoskins, would have to step very small before Fox forgot that drenching crab.

As it was Lieutenant Lionel Grey, sitting at Fox's side in the sternsheets, called out: "Damn you, stroke! If you can't pull an oar by now I'll have you scraping gumboe, you useless blagskitel"

Fox let the byplay drift by. Grey was his first lieutenant and was entitled to curse and blast if the crew did not perform adequately. And, Lionel Grey knew Fox's ways by now—or some of them—and would know that Fox strained always for that perfect ideal that any sane man knew was impossible. Yet, being Fox, he would always go on striving.

He would have Grey as his first, a young lieutenant called Alfred Blythe as his second, and there were three master's mates. As for midshipmen, Staunton had written to congratulate him, and had with the utmost tact suggested that Fox might care to ship Mr. Midshipman Gruber. It was done delicately; but Fox did not miss the undertones. If Percy Staunton had for a space given up the sea and turned to his lordly estates, he had put in his oar to assist Fox and was now requesting payment by finding a place for Gruber. What Gruber's Interest was, Fox did not know. Why Staunton should wish the lad to sail with an old tarpaulin like Fox instead of with some smart frigate captain escaped him; but he welcomed Gruber. Fox had little time for most people; for those in whom he found that spark he recognized as of worth he would go out of his way. He looked to Midshipman Gruber as a lad who might turn out well. Like Grey, for example.

Fox had discovered that Grey's promotion to lieutenant had taken place a week after John Carker's. He had tried to get Carker; but a lowly newly made commander had no real powers in that direction. John Carker had been found employment and had shipped out as a third of *Narcissus*. Just when, or if ever, Fox would see Carker again remained obscure.

It would be strange having Grey as his immediate subordinate. Always before there had been Carker between them.

Felix Gruber stood ready to shout an immediate warning of the jolly boat's approach. The assistant-master, Watson, a second master who would through courtesy usually be referred to by all aboard as the master, was on his toes. Fox would look to him for professional competence and assistance before the second lieutenant, Alfred Blythe.

Everything kept insisting on happening in a confused melange of events, with nothing in order, no ordered sequence of happenings; but he did not care. He knew exactly what he was doing. He had been enormously fortunate. *Minion* had been in commission, no doubt occupied in the work for which she had been built, and her crew had had time to settle down. Or so Fox imagined. Her recent captain, a commander Thompson, and his first lieutenant, Mr. Hyde, had both left the ship; one to take command of a sheer hulk, the other to rot on the beach. Fox did not know the reasons for this, and he pushed away any ominous thoughts that occurred to him. He'd have welcomed the command of a sheer hulk himself, at times; any command was better than frittering life away ashore.

The upshot was that he and Grey were taking command of a vessel and crew intactum. There would be no desperate measures to find hands. He would cast a most severe eye over the purser's accounts, and the records of all the standing officers would be most minutely scrutinized; but he had been spared the problems of fitting out and manning.

The devil of it was *Minion* was short-handed. Trying to find a ship in the service that was not under-manned was a game of needle-in-the-haystack, although a good captain with first class connections might be able to complete more or less to his satisfaction. *Minion* most certainly had not completed to Fox' satisfaction.

With eighteen weapons and ostensibly a complement of over a hundred, a hundred and twenty-one was the figure in theory never reached in practice, she was a sloop and a commander's command, although by definition a gun-boat by function. With two extra weapons she would become a sixth rate and then would need a post captain to command, and my lords commissioners of the Admiralty were not foolish enough to make a mistake like that. Even the big twenty-carronade gun-boats were still not sixth rates.

And some of them were larger than the more elderly twenty-eight gun frigates.

The jolly boat surged up and down in that awkward cross sea. Fox could observe the sudden activity on *Minion*'s flush deck—thought of that did not please him, either—and by the time the bowman hooked on and Fox could spring up on deck everything was ready to welcome the captain aboard.

Truth to tell—and to hell with any feelings of guilty pride—he took an immense delight in naval honors thus bestowed on him. They meant nothing, of course, to any man who thought about these things; but what they did do they did splendidly. They made it abundantly plain that the man stepping aboard and for whom all this fuss was made was the captain, the god almighty in the ship, and let that same fear inspire everyone to their duty, or God help 'em.

"Bigod!" said Grey, hunching forward and staring with lowering brows upon *Minion*. "She's an ugly bitch. I'll wager a year's pay she's a damned poor sailer, lay me horizontal else."

"Aye, Mr. Grey. Ugly she may be, and a damned poor sailer too, into the bargain. But she's a job to do, and she'll do that job." Fox jerked his head at the row of closed gun-ports, eight of them cut large for the carronades, and the one up in the bow for the six-pounder. "She has teeth, Mr. Grey. Now pray we get outselves a Frog to sink those teeth into."

"Amen to that, sir."

Thought of those massive but relatively light thirty-two pounder carronades put Fox into a slightly more jocular frame of mind, a dash of bubbles bursting up over his

70

good mood. Once upon a time he'd foolishly hankered after twenty-four-pounder guns; he'd come to the conclusion that at around fifty hundredweight the saving of thirteen hundredweight in the weight of the twenty-four pounders as against thirty-two pounders did not offset their lesser punch, for they were just as big and clumsy to move around. And the eighteen-pounders at around forty-two hundredweights were a useful weapon. He'd seen the differences serving in many ships, most notably latterly in *Hector*, which as an eighty, had shipped twenty-four pounders in place of the eighteens of a seventy-four. No, he'd decided that the thirty-two pounder was not so much more difficult to manage than a twenty-four pounder and therefore was the gun of the future.

Now, although they were carronades and not guns, he had sixteen of the beauties to play with. In a navy which devoutly believed in the doctrine of close-action battle, the heavy-shotted carronade was a blessing. Fox still harbored doubts; he hankered still after that mythical ship of his equipped with a big and powerful long range gun. But that, he fancied, belonged in the same world as that inhabited by his poetic friends who lived shoreside.

In the vessels of the navy of such small dimensions as these brigs and sloops and schooners and cutters, all manner of varieties in arming were to be found. An ordinary eighteen gun sloop shipped eighteen six-pounders. But then, *Minion* was of that kind of gun-brig armed with carronades designed to get in at the enemy. There would be no convoy work for him, no Inshore Squadron work with the blockading forces, not much despatch work. He knew where he was going. It was up to him to see *Minion* was capable of doing the work for which she had been designed.

And if, in the course of those duties, *Minion* was de-

71

stroyed, why, then, the service and the country would have lost one small and insignificant vessel, a few carronades, and a tiny crew that might be swept up in an hour during a hot press in any town.

So, why, with all the glory of a new command should his confounded infallible memory go back to Tunbridge Wells?

That last morning, before the letter from Cloughton had arrived to change everything, he had bumped into Lord Kintlesham. The old peer, as vague, as bumbling, had been as kind as ever, kindness itself. They had talked of those rattling days in *Raccoon*, shipping the marbles back to safety from the barbarian French. Fox knew this to be ludicrous nonsense and Kintlesham, too, for his part as an antiquarian, had been full of praise for the work of the French antiquaries. But, and here the old insular pride showed through, he'd expressed himself as being damned first if he'd allow any rascally Revolutionary to lay his hands on a single priceless relic of the ancient world.

Fox had got the course of the conversation onto Sophy.

Kintlesham's long face grew longer and he banged his cane onto the tiles beneath the long canopy of the Upper Walk.

"Sophy is like a painted butterfly, these days, Mr. Fox. And as miserable as sin. I tell you, sir, she is hell to live with." And then Kintlesham had added: "I admit my regrets, my dear Mr. Fox, that some further accommodation was not reached between my daughter and your self, for I own, sir, she is a changed girl." He chuckled rather like the main chain-pump of a hundred gun three-decker. "Woman, rather."

They walked together in the sunshine, from the Pump Room and along, with the shops on their right hand, with the morning people working themselves up for the day's fray, toward the far end where they would give themselves over to the delights to be found there. Jennie was met, and introduced, and Kintlesham bumbled and burbled and contrived to remember a mutual acquaintance from Leicestershire, and enquired after Jack Blane, and things were going swimmingly when Sophy appeared.

She stood, half in sunshine half in shadow, one hand supporting herself on a colonnade pillar. What noises were going on, Fox could not tell. The music from the little wooden pavilion perched opposite the colonnade, birds singing, the wind sighing, people laughing and chattering all about—he heard none of these noises, if these noises even existed.

Sophy cut him dead.

She walked past affecting not to see her father's stare, and took his arm, and broke into some inane airy morning chatter. Her face had rushed with scarlet at sight of Fox; now she was deathly pale. But that meant nothing. Lord Kintlesham tried to turn, to bow, to say something, and Sophy fairly dragged him away.

"The painted bitch!" said Jennie, feelingly.

Fox did not say anything.

When she had been all fat and red and sweaty she had sighed for love of him and wanted him; now she was gorgeous and alluring and she detested him.

Sophy!

In his tiny cramped cabin in *Minion* he knew why he had been so unpleasantly reminded of what he had thought to put out of his mind, for Mr. Grey had been talking of *Raccoon*.

"Now if *Minion* was like *Raccoon*!" Grey had spoken with all the fire of an enthusiast over a lost love. So there had been that double reason to allow forbidden thoughts into his head. *Raccoon*, that beautiful brig he'd commanded as a lieutenant temporarily and for such a short time in the Mediterranean, was such a vessel as did not often come the way of humble commanders, and the miracle was that he'd even smelt her at all. *Minion* might be a sea cow, but . . .

"It is not, Mr. Grey!"

Grey glanced at his captain in some amazement.

"We are in *Minion,* Mr. Grey, and we have a deal to do to turn her into a vessel I would wish to command, for I sense an underlying current here, Mr. Grey, of corruption and defeat. But, you forget, I think, that *Raccoon* is no more than a heap of blackened ashes."

"Yes, sir, I—that is—"

Fox knew what Grey meant. But he was back to being Fox again, and all the silly chit-chat of a fashionable spa lay behind him. They were sea officers about the king's business. And that business was sticky and fraught and would be highly unpleasant and dangerous.

"Very well, Mr. Grey. You'll greatly oblige me by reporting to me just as soon as you can get under way." Fox lifted his head to glare at Grey. Lieutenant Lionel Grey was no longer Mr. Midshipman Grey. But at the ice cold look in Fox's eyes he touched his hat, swung about, and went out of that tiny cabin and up onto the quarterdeck as though the imps of hell were after him.

Minion was flush decked and so the after end of the deck had been arbitrarily declared to be the quarterdeck. From the taffrail to the shrouds of the mainmast extended the area which, on *Minion* at least, was dubbed the quarterdeck. Fox's cabin, cramped, angled with the run of the ship's lines, so low that even he had to incline his head, remained still the most impressive cabin aboard. *Minion* possessed a single deck supporting her artillery. Everything had been sacrificed to those damn great carronades.

74

Her people slept and messed and had their being on platforms with a bare five feet of headroom, and the floor below housed stores crammed in like cherries into a jar. She had but the one deck. The rest was a mish-mash of platforms. Fox felt that, although somewhat larger than *Clothilde*, which brig he had taken from the French only to have her bottom fall out—just like *Imperieuse!*—*Minion* would be an even worse sailer. She would go to leeward like a rice pudding on ice.

So. He was in command. He had a job to do. He had a vessel to lick into the shape his intolerant search after perfection might find acceptable. That would mean first discovering what canker it was that ate at this crew; for no sea officer of Fox's experience could have failed to miss the betraying signs in the crew's demeanor. He had often wondered if some black bastard had not deliberately set fire to *Queen Charlotte*. A first rate three-decker of a hundred guns should not go up in flames killing 673 of her people after five hours of fire fighting before the explosion of her magazines. That terrible news still had power to shock, and it had only happened on the seventeenth of March. If some blagskite tried to set fire to *Minion*, why, then, Fox would—Fox would—well, hell, Fox would be exceedingly unpleasant to him.

With the money he had won he had managed to set himself up tolerably comfortably, laying in poultry, wine, fresh vegetables, a barrel of eggs—if they lasted he'd take back what he'd sworn—and all the tea he could afford. He'd spent on his command, also, as any captain must. He had absolutely turned his back on providing gold leaf. He knew what the pundits said of gold leaf, that a little spread around the ship spread also news of a captain's concern for his command; Fox had spread a little cash around and had in the ways of the Navy bought extra kegs of gunpowder—and good fresh stuff, too, none of your filthy reconstituted rubbish, either. His cabin furnishings were of spartan simplicity. They included a mirror.

Now, for the first time since coming aboard, and just as Grey knocked and came into the cabin past the marine sentry, who was, Fox considered, a reasonable investment, he looked into that mirror in its walnut stand. His reflection stared back.

Yes.

Oh, indeed, yes!

It glittered in the lanternlight—for this cabin boasted no array of great stern windows—it flashed and scintillated and, as God was his witness, quite a lot of it was real bullion.

It hung there on his left shoulder, a damn great shining, glorious, refulgent, altogether wonderful creation of the gods of destiny.

Oh, yes, indeed and truly yes, it was wonderful to be alive.

"All ready to get under way, sir," said Mr. Grey with stiff formality.

"Very good, Mr. Grey. I will come on deck."

He took one last long look. Damn Grey—for the whipper did not have this golden glorious epaulette hanging from his left shoulder!

And so, with a final hitch of his shoulder, for he still felt lopsided, and with a flaunting swing from his swab, Commander George Abercrombie Fox went up on deck to take his command, *Minion*, to sea.

CHAPTER SEVEN

Commander Fox stared with some acerbity through the overcast night up Roulet inlet, and whilst both of those treacherous eyes of his were working satisfactorily, he had the itchy feeling that at any moment now that damned filthy ring of purple and black would come hemming in the vision of his left eye. He peered with his head jutting forward, his old horror of a hat jammed onto his brown hair which, in the fashion, was cut in some fashionable disarray, glaring past *Minion's* bowsprit and up the inlet where, if intelligence of lobster-pot men and spies and anyone who would blab for gold was to be believed, two French schooners and a lugger lay moored.

Minion ghosted forward gently in the night, her reefed topsails shivering slightly, all her noises muted, with the oiled blocks whispering rather than screeching, her timbers groaning in a mumbling sotto voce, the breeze barely tickling her rigging. The water tinkled loudly from her forefoot.

She rode a little down by the head, which made her

performance that much more tricky when tacking, and there had been no time to balance out her weights, with everything jammed so vigorously into space for which it had not been designed.

"Keep your eyes peeled there," said Fox in a low and cutting whisper that reached forward to the lookout and no farther.

The man lifted a hand in response, obeying Fox's vicious orders about silent discipline. If a man spoke out of turn now he'd be flogged stupid. Already the hands realized they had caught a tartar in Commander Fox.

He'd joined the tiny flotilla commanded by Captain Benjamin Dawson in *Boadicea*, thirty-two, to no pomp or circumstance, no heaven-revealing joy that a brand new commander had brought his command from England to the French coast. There was another gun-brig, smaller and with only ten thirty-two pounder carronades and therefore fit for a lieutenant's command. Lieutenant Forbes, a dour Yorkshireman, had her. There was an armed cutter, *Folly*, with acting lieutenant Simpson in command, who no doubt considered himself the luckiest young devil alive. Apart from the swab on his left shoulder, Fox could see the young man's point of view, particularly when, as now, he was going into action with a ship's company who were, to say the least, not happy with either life or their vessel.

Minion followed *Darter*, Forbes' gun-brig, and was in turn followed by a collection of boats from *Boadicea* and the other two sloops that made up the squadron. These were real sloops, deep-water vessels, able to sail to the Antipodes if needs be. They were not, however, suitable for the kind of work in which *Minion* and *Darter* were now engaged. So they sent their boats and their first lieutenants, and Mr. Algernon Faulkner, first of *Boadicea*, taking his place in *Darter*, led the procession up the night-shrouded inlet. Fox wasn't too sure that he approved of this arrangement; but Captain Dawson had made it very plain that he was not a man to be trifled with.

The huddle of boats following the brigs pulled steadily on. Fox looked at his canvas. If the breeze grew more flukey he'd have the yards stripped and the men at the sweeps. There were seven oar ports aside, in line with the gun-ports of the single deck. Fox knew very well what the men thought of those oar-ports, and of the labor required to drag the heavy sweeps through the water. He'd spare them that until there was no other course.

If the blagskites thought he spared them out of pity, or from humane considerations, they were wrong, ludicrously wrong. He just did not want to tire the hands before they got into action. He had come to certain conclusions about his new command. He fancied the canker stemmed from a number of conjoined reasons, of which the most obvious should not have been allowed any pressure on the hands whatsoever. The brig was small and slow and ugly and un-lovely, and she was abominable in any sort of sea because of her shallow draught, and her accommodation was worse even than normal in a King's Ship. She was wet so that the hands, once their clothes were drenched, and that would happen the first night out, could never get dry again. Her victuals were appalling. Yet these conditions were perfectly normal. Fox had endured them all his sea-faring life. It was just, in this area, that *Minion* was that little bit worse than the men cared for. In these small vessels the discomforts of this kind rested heavily where in, say, a seventy-four, there were ways and means of circumventing them.

But, given all that, there was something else amiss.

As *Minion* stole stealthily up the Roulet inlet beneath a starless sky, following the shielded light of *Darter* ahead,

Fox deliberately let his thoughts range upon other facts and fancies than this cold onward movement. He fancied, and was almost sure, that the ship's corporal, one Harvey, a man robust and alert and large, with a fierce lowering face with that shagreen look about it that so revolted Fox, remembering that vile Master-at-Arms, Mr. Doherty, was at the bottom of *Minion's* troubles. The Purser had the man written up fair in the muster book. He'd been a Master-at-Arms, himself, and had been broken for an offense which, minor though it might be, was one not to be tolerated in the ship's officer charged with discipline, for he had succumbed to extra rum and other foibles and had conspired to cheat justice of a villainous boatswain. Mr. Harvey, as was, had been broken and, as part of his punishment, had been degraded in rank and sent aboard a King's Ship as a landman.

Commander Thompson, the last captain of *Minion*, had seen fit to rate him ship's corporal. Fox had a shrewd idea of what was going on aboard, and guessed no one had as yet screwed up their courage to talk. Or—had they? Was that why Thompson and his first lieutenant had been sent out of the ship?

Immediately on reporting to Captain Dawson of *Boadicea* Fox and *Minion* had been sent on this present dangerous night duty. All the time Fox stood on his very own quarterdeck, miniscule though it might be, and standing thus he did not cease from—as the standing orders would phrase it—taking stock of his surroundings and estimating elapsed time, and the drift of the current and tide, the way the wind shifted, and the high loom of the clouds covering the starless sky, the tiny dot of light ahead that was *Darter's* signal, the sense of the boats following his own stern light. And, all the time, he kept his ugly lump of a face compressed into a hideous scowl that effectively prevent-

80

ed Mr. Grey from opening a conversation for Grey, by this time, knew when to and when not to speak to his captain.

A captain could rate a petty officer and could therefore derate him. Yet Fox did not wish simply to dispose of Harvey without cause, for the man would still be aboard and although deprived of his police position would still be stronger and tougher and more vicious than any of them, and so well able to maintain his position as cock of the walk.

And—if anyone suggested *Minion* was a dunghill then they would answer to George Abercrombie Fox at their peril.

Darter's light flickered twice.

"Very good, Mr. Grey," said Fox before Grey could report.

But Grey, in whose hands of necessity much of the running of the vessel now lay, could give the next order and soon *Minion's* stern light flickered twice. Immediately thereafter and to whispered orders which, at night, always produced a most powerful effect, *Minion's* canvas was got in. She glided on under her own momentum for a space and then, again to those eerie whispered orders, the sweeps were unshipped and the brig eased along to the pull of fourteen blades biting through the water. Fox felt some approval. He had got his sweeps out perhaps that little in advance; but he had wished to use what he could of residual momentum. To start the vessel under way from rest was a herculean task, and one which he wished to spare his men.

"Keep her as she goes," he said in that fierce sotto voce to the helmsman. The tiller had been well greased and moved silently. For this kind of work a tiller was a tremendous advantage, giving an immediate bite and response from the rudder that even the best wheel and cylinder arrangement could never give because of the slack in the ropes.

Now Fox thought he could make out the loom of land ahead. He would have preferred to lead, but *Darter* drew eighteen inches less than *Minion*.

The boats came surging up from astern and their oars, pulling in neat geometrical rhythm, drove them past. Fox saw the dark splotches of uniforms, and the white splotches of faces, and the vaguer splotches of greyness in the boats where the marines sat clumped together in the center. His marines were there, somewhere, and Gruber, God help him, was there, also.

Now the land was unmistakable.

He could make out nothing of what lay below that vague band of darker grey against the sky. Grey was peering with that fierce contained look on his face that had accompanied all the violent actions they had been in together. He wondered what John Carker, the third of *Narcissus*, was doing now, and then concentrated exclusively on what was happening ahead.

Up there lay two schooners and a lugger. They were of little force for this expedition; but on the Petit Mallou the French had constructed a battery armed with half a dozen thirty-six-pounders. The Petit Mallou, a shallow island almost connected to the mainland at low tide, dominated a tricky right-angled bend. Once past there the French shipping would be at the mercy of the British; but the raiding party would be at the mercy of the battery.

Fox was a man who liked things to go the way he desired. They very often did not; that would not prevent him from always attempting to order things to his desires. He could see that an assault on the Petit Mallou battery would clear the way for the return. But he misdoubted the whole concept of the plan. Captain Dawson had had no doubts, and it ill-befitted a lowly and new-appointed commander to argue with a senior post captain flaunting two gold epaulettes. Fox would so do his damnedest as he always did to win.

"And a quarter less five!" whispered Partridge, the master's mate assigned the task of repeating the leadsman's call to Fox.

Almost immediately Partridge was saying: "By the deep four!"

G. A. Fox was prepared to take *Minion* into two fathoms.

He was not prepared to venture further than that. As he had once been told with much gravity and shaking of the head by Captain Sir Cuthbert Rowlands, than whom there had been no captain worthier the name: "A sailor, Fox, who wishes to remain afloat and alive will place caution before foolhardiness." And then, because Fox was Fox and well-known to Captain Rowlands, he had added: "And it takes courage to be cautious, my lad, so learn your lesson."

The boats had all pulled ahead and vanished. *Darter's* stern light shone bravely in that narrow funnel made by the concealing sideboards.

"By the mark three!"

The leadsman would have in his wet fingers the dripping leather marker with the three ends. Fox remained immobile. Now he could see a faint scattering of lights beneath the land. Impossible to distinguish shipping from here, as it would be impossible for the French to pick out the two English gun-vessels bearing down on them. The hands swung and swayed at the sweeps, and Grey took a quick trip forward on the larboard side and aft on the starboard side to make sure that Mr. Macmillan, the

83

boatswain, and the master's mate assigned to that task, Mr. Kilmartin, had the men well under control and together. The master shuffled a little and then froze, remaining dumb. Fox stood hunched up, his arrogantly-beaked face peering into the night.

"By the mark three!"

Minion moved smoothly ahead under the impetus of her sweeps. Then Fox made out the break in the channel. Without turning his head, he said: "Mr. Watson. Would you kindly take us around with plenty of sea room."

That was a babblement for Fox; but this was his first command that was truly his, for *Raccoon* had been on sufferance only. Away to starboard the land stretched now, darker and more solid, and that scattering of lights brightened. On the larboard side hung the darkling water, for the inlet of the Roulet widened here until it formed a wide but shallow pool. Over on the larboard side only darkness met his eyes. Watson gave his orders in that eerie harsh whisper and the hands at the tillers, for Fox had had men posted at the second tiller that defaced his own cabin, eased the brig around so that she swung on rudder alone to starboard. That was the sensible way of doing it, so that the long rhythm of the men at the sweeps was not interrupted.

"Damme, Capt'n Fox!" said the Master. "It's blacker than the Duke of Hell's riding boots!"

Fox did not forbear to answer that.

They swung now to starboard and Mr. Partridge was saying: "And a quarter less three!"

Fox had to allow for *Minion* riding with her forefoot deeper than it should. By the time the leadsman had coiled his line, heaved the lead, waited for the onward movement of the vessel to bring the line plumb, and then felt what marker or absence of marker lay under his fingers, called out his findings for Partridge to repeat, *Minion* would have gone so far through the water that the bottom could have shelved into a beach.

"Ease her, Mr. Watson. Starboard your helm."

"Starboard your helm it is, sir."

Minion eased to larboard.

The charts of the Roulet inlet were probably foully out of date and inaccurate; but they were all he had had to go on. They nestled in his head in that compartment reserved for the charts of all the places in the world he had served, aye, and places to which he had not yet travelled. Once they were past this shallow lagoon they would be up with the moorings of the schooners and the lugger. At that moment a cacophony of shots and crashes and the fainter yells of men in mortal combat erupted from the Petit Mallou.

Fox looked back.

Flashes lit the night sky over the island, and then a whole series of sparking illuminations. Someone was firing volleys over there, and it wouldn't be either the French or the British Jack Tars. That was the marines in action.

Minion prowled on, and: "By the deep four!"

The next cast of the lead brought: "And a half four!"

"Thank God for that," remarked Mr. Watson of no one in particular.

How easy for Fox to have said: "Thank God when we've safely gone through two fathoms, Mr. Watson." But he did not speak. He had been pitchforked into action at too early a stage in his developing awareness of *Minion*. So he took what was in any event an easy course and adopted the pose of the silent captain. Later they'd get the rough edge of his tongue, bigod! They would!

The plan called for *Darter's* boats—she had two of

85

them, mere cockleshells—to carry the French ships. If they could not be taken out then they would be burned. As always, Fox had felt a saturnine relief that he was not to be called on to burn a ship.

As a Commander he outranked Lieutenant Forbes, *Darter's* captain; but Captain Dawson knowing Forbes and knowing nothing of Fox had entrusted that part of the operation to the man he knew, and had got around the seniority problem by informing Fox that he was in command of the 'covering force'. Fox took the charge seriously.

It meant that he was responsible for stopping anyone interfering with Forbes, and of getting the expedition safely out.

Those words ghosted up as *Minion* ran on under her sweeps.

"Hereof nor you nor any of ye may fail, as you will answer the contrary at your Peril."

Punishment was savage and merciless. Rewards were not as swift, were far from generous, most uncertain and reserved only for the completely successful.

Lights showed ahead and for a moment Fox lost *Darter's* stern lantern. He picked it up in the same second that the French began firing from the shore. Fox looked steadfastly at the tongues of flame lashing from the darkness. Smoke which he could not see made the flames leap and dance, disappearing and appearing like graveyard ghouls and will-o'-the-wisps dancing an obscene saraband. He saw the pattern.

Grey swung about, and all pretense of silence was lost.

"That's a frigate, sir! A forty-four or I'm a Dutchman!"

"Aye, Mr. Grey. And he's shooting twenty-four-pounders."

"So what happened to our intelligence? Why were we not informed that besides schooners and luggers there is a damned great French frigate up the Roulet?"

This was Grey's first taste of action as the first lieutenant of a vessel. Fox watched him calmly. Grey was a man in whom he felt he could repose the utmost of confidence that Fox was prepared to trust in anyone. But if Grey carried on like this . . . And then Lionel Grey realized where he was and what he was doing, and the moment passed, and he was once more the calm and yet dashing lieutenant of an English vessel of war.

"We've only carronades, sir," said Lieutenant Alfred Blythe. He appeared on the quarterdeck, touching his hat, preparing to go on speaking.

Fox regarded him in astonishment.

"What are you doing here, Mr. Blythe?"

Blythe swallowed in his eagerness.

"I came aft, sir, to request permission to open fire with the six-pounders—"

Fox opened his mouth to let rip a string of abuse, of a blinding roaring cursing rip-roaring avalanche of invective that would cow and smash this second lieutenant of his. But, instead, and in the nick of time, he adopted that hateful, low, cutting, deadly voice, to say: "You were not given my leave to lay aft, Mr. Blythe. You were not given my permission to desert your post forrard. I shall not overlook this insubordination, Mr. Blythe. Now get forrard, instanter!"

Blythe looked absolutely stricken.

He swung about to go.

"And, Mr. Blythe, you may not open fire with your six-pounder popguns. Is that understood?"

"Aye aye, sir."

Blythe dare say no more.

No shouts had reached *Minion*. Fox had no wish to have thirty-six pound shot—no doubt heated into red-hot rounds of fiery destruction—hurtling about the fragile scantlings of his new vessel. A thinning and shredding of clouds let a few pinpricks of light down, and rockets soared from the French coastline. In the pale illumination Fox could see the ghostly leap of water spouts alongside the dark bulk of *Darter*, and he saw her maintopmast plunge overside. His ugly face went uglier still.

Minion was creeping along under her sweeps, yet with that thinning of the cloud a little breeze gusted down the Roulet. All hope of surprise was now gone. The night air quivered to the shock of gunfire. The Petit Mallou still showed that flickering musketry although the bangings had faded with distance. So the fort had not yet been taken. He thought of Gruber and he wondered what dire hangings and quarterings would follow if he smashed his mahogany-hard fist into the face of Lieutenant Algernon Faulkner, first of *Boadicea*, aboard *Darter*, or in the face of the officer responsible for the fiasco on the Petit Mallou, or into the face of Captain Dawson, who was responsible for this mess.

But then, the intelligence had been false. The French had no doubt hoodwinked the British and installed an agent in one of their innocent-seeming lobster boats. It was no use worrying over spilt milk. The whole coast was aflame, a forty-four twenty-four-pounder frigate was blasting their consort out of the water, a six-gun battery of thirty-sixes in their rear remained unsubdued, and, as commander of the covering force, Commander George Abercrombie Fox had now to prove his right to wear that flaunting golden epaullette on his left shoulder.

"Mr. Grey!" he bawled in his roaring Foxey style. "In sweeps! Top's'ls and t'garns!" Then, in his Bull of Bashan bellow, forward along the deck: "Stand to your guns!" He roared his orders, filling the cannon-rumbling night with savagery. "Jib and stays'ls! Mr. Watson! Port your helm! We're going down to give those Frogs a little medicine, and I devoutly trust it'll make 'em sicker than a month-pregnant woman! Jump to it, you evil heap o' blagskites! Let's see what you Minions are made of!"

CHAPTER EIGHT

Commander Fox stared with both his evil ice-cold eyes functioning perfectly as the hands raced aloft to shake out the topsails and the topgallants. He wasn't bothering with courses; for one thing the Roulet tended to chop off lower airs. Equally, he wasn't going to bother with any nonsense about royals at this juncture. He watched malevolently as Grey roared into the men, yelling his orders in ways that he had learned in his previous commissions with Fox. A series of rustling flaps and sudden bangings as odd folds shook out and the sails hung. The men hustled to clear the yards.

"We're fore reaching on *Darter,* sir," reported Mr. Watson.

Fox peered forward through the luridly-lit night. Yes. There was no doubt of it. *Darter* was hauling her wind. She had lost her foremast, the whole shebang, foremast, foretop mast and foretopgallant mast, all gone. In the flicker of reflected light off the water and the bursting pyrotechnics of French rockets, Fox saw lithe agitated figures hanging onto *Darter's* forechains with one hand and slashing and hacking with axes in the other. Their frenzied movements were all of a piece with the night's action.

Orange streaks reflected from the water runnels. A white spout lifted magically a cable's length away. *Minion* was now gliding toward the shore, between *Darter* and the shore, between *Darter* and the French frigate.

Before he heard Grey swearing insanely Fox sensed trouble. A party of waisters were hauling and getting nowhere. The boatswain's mate was lashing them with his starter; a halyard had jammed in a sheave and the block wouldn't budge. Then Fox saw something that might, in other circumstances, have made him smile. He wondered why men came to sea and risked their necks against the elements and other men in fire and blood and storm; but seeing Grey as he flung himself forward, stopped the mate from his stupid belaboring, and then sorted out the jammed block, made Fox understand a little more of the reasons why other men came to sea. For himself, it was a case of that or starve.

The block freed and with a squeal the yard rose. Instantly the hands tailed onto the sheets and sheeted home. The braces swung the yards exactly as Fox wanted. He let Grey set up the angle and merely corrected it by a quarter point. *Minion* now picked up that flukey wind and, gentle as was the breeze, with her shallow build she leaned over as she picked up way.

Darter had been firing, of course; but Fox doubted if any of her shot reached. If only some magnificent genius could invent a gun that carried the weight of a carronade for its lightness! As it was, you had practically to stick yourself eyeball to eyeball with carronades. Fox did not believe in the yard-arm to yard-arm theory so popular in

91

the Navy. But he was stuck with it now, and with a vengeance!

So *Minion* rolled down to battle.

The last time Fox had trod a quarterdeck and taken a ship into action had been different bigod! Then he'd been in an eighty-gun ship of the line, and in practical command of four ships of the line. Now he comamnded a scrawny little brig and was in for a hiding to nothing against a frigate he'd have blown out of the water with his magnificent eighty.

A ship's boy, one of the four second class boys the manning scheme allowed them, hauled up at Fox's bellow.

"My compliments to Mr. Blythe on the fo'c'sle, younker. Mr. Blythe to lay aft. On the double now, lad."

The little rabbit squeak spouted up: "Aye aye, sir."

The lad ran off, his long trousers cut halfway up his calves, his feet bare, his shirt tattered. His face looked the face of a little mouse peering from the wainscotting. He needed a damn good meal and less attention from Mr. Harvey.

With Mr. Midshipman Gruber out of the vessel Fox was bereft of middies, a deficiency he in normal times would have welcomed, being a sour old dog. Now he would have to make shift. Alfred Blythe appeared, his face still showing signs of his last encounter with this maniacal captain.

"You will take command of the main battery, Mr. Blythe. Open fire when I so command. And, Mr. Blythe, I do not wish to observe any carronade fire early—or late —and I do not wish to observe any miss. You will convey my sentiments in the matter to the quarter gunners. I do not care how many men are given red-checked shirts at the gratings. Do I make myself clear?"

"Aye aye, sir." Blythe swallowed.

He scuttled off. In the mad dash to get his vessel into enemy waters and duly reported to Captain Dawson, Fox had had no time to assess his new crew beyond the recognition of that canker that any experienced sea officer would have spotted instantly. He had done so. But there had been no time to do anything about it. And now they were in action with a crew on whom he felt the utmost reluctance to rely. Yet he had to go down in flame and smoke to action and trust that the immemorial traditions of the Royal Navy, instilled by rum and the lash, would hold these men together.

It really wasn't good enough for George Abercrombie Fox, bigod!

Grey came up. "She's firing all her broadside, sir." He put his handsome silver watch back into his fob pocket. "Ten seconds over three minutes, sir, I am happy to say."

"Very good, Mr. Grey." Fox felt a bubbling lift of pleasure. Grey had been timing the French broadsides. That encouraged Fox. But he had to sound a note of warning. Privacy on so small a vessel was almost out of the question, except perhaps to a low-voiced conversation in the captain's cabin; or, as now, except during an action. "We do not know the caliber of our gun crews, Mr. Grey. I would wish to have had them go through the drill at least once."

Grey absorbed that. He nodded. Then he brightened. "She's been in commission a year, sir. They must have drilled into some likely shape."

Fox did not have to answer that and so did not.

Now *Darter* lay broad on their larboard beam. She looked a mess, without a foremast and with only her mainmast standing. Forbes had the sweeps out and was laboriously attempting to turn his vessel. The coast lay still in darkness; a few lights clustered here and there. Then the long orange tongues of flame lashed from the French frigate. She was lying moored, head and stern, a dark lump of menace against the darkness. She would have all her ample crew manning her one broadside, and they would be ready to smash any feeble attempt at boarding by the undermanned *Minion*.

"By God!" said Fox as the shot came in. "We'll sink our teeth in the bastard."

As usual the French aimed high and with a little of the luck that so often frowned on Fox, nothing vital was shot away. Grey went at the boatswain to start splicing and knotting. *Minion* surged on. Fox felt his hands clenching. Being on the same level as the gun crews was no new experience, for had he not served on the lower gun deck of, for example, *Tiger*? But he missed that trick of being able to grip the quarterdeck rail and lean over and bawl at the upturned faces of the gun crews. Still, he bawled all the same.

"Open fire as your guns bear. I want every shot to count!"

"Aye aye, sir!" came Blythe's answering shout.

From the bow rippling on like a breaking wave of thunder the carronades fired from *Minion's* starboard side. That enormous discharge was heralded by the banging of the fore six-pounder. Fox counted. At the count of four the expected concussion did not occur and the carronade did not rear back on its slide. The next carronade took up the drum roll and so thay smashed and roared aft. Fox looked along the deck where the smoke blew stingingly. One duff one out of eight. Now to see what kind of gun discipline Commander Thompson had kept aboard the vessel from which he had been dismissed.

The minutes ticked by. Fox watched the nearest gun crew. They worked hard. There was no doubt about that.

A carronade could be worked by two men, as the merchantmen had found out to their comfort before the navy had taken up the carronade. Three men to the aft thirty-two-pounder carronade were taking one hell of a time to reload. At Fox's side Grey had his watch nonchalantly held in his fingers. Then the frigate fired again and Fox heard that death's-knell whicker as shot passed above. *Minion* shuddered and a tremendous smashing shook her from forward. Men were screaming up there.

For a few moments pandemonium threatened.

Grey cast a glance at Fox. Still the forward carronade had not fired again and nearly three minutes had elapsed. Fox returned the stare with icy calm. He had no means at the moment to discern what damage, if any, they had had inflicted on the frigate. He did not wish to take any way off his command. He would need all the speed he could muster to go about.

Grey said: "Permission to go forrard, sir, and—"

The rest of his words were drowned in the crash of the second carronade, and then the others went off at different times and intervals. It was not so disgraceful a display as might be imagined, for this was normal when a broadside was in action as the quicker crews worked to a faster tempo; the fault was that it should happen so early.

Grey had the sense not to bother to repeat his remarks. The carronades would fire, after a fashion and in their own time. Fox stood quietly fuming. He had lost count of the times he had drilled a ship's gun-crews. He had thrashed many and many a team into being. But to have to take his first drills live, to time his men as they were in action, that was an insult he wouldn't forget.

The breeze came off the shore over *Minion's* starboard beam so that her smoke swept away to larboard. Fox looked back. He could just make out *Darter,* a looming mass, and she looked as though she had barely moved. Forbes had better get something working over there, or even Fox wouldn't be able to assist him. Over on his starboard side the frigate had passed away aft. Each vessel had fired two broadsides. The damage to *Minion* was slight, although three men had been killed, their blood greasy on the deck, their brains a slippery trap for the feet of their shipmates.

Fox had the position as effortlessly worked out in his head as he worked out everything. *Minion* headed on the starboard tack up the Roulet. Behind her on her larboard lay *Darter*, struggling with sweeps to turn herself. And to her starboard lay the French frigate with her hungry twenty-four-pounder guns anxious to blast the English sloop into driftwood. There was room—just. The currents and set of the tide had to be figured in, and the leadsman would be able to yell at full strength, so that would be a relief from all the conspirational whispering.

Fox waited.

The carpenter reported all well with the well. The purser reported the deaths of the three seamen. No one else was so much as scratched. A single stray shot had done for them, clustered at a carronade. Mr. Blythe had remanned the piece with a fresh crew.

Grey was looking at Fox in the dimness and Fox knew exactly what was in that young imp of satan's mind. How odd to know that in all probability Grey would be posted as a captain before Fox, that he might be under the lad's orders one day, and that not too far into the future!

The master, Mr. Watson, was harrumphing away. Yet already he had become aware that one did not speak lightly to Commander Fox. They must wonder what he was about. Tht boatswain came up to report the hawser led through aft and made ready. If he was going to have to

96

tow *Darter* out he had no wish to have to rush about making preparations at the last minute.

"Very good." Fox wasn't going to be fulsome to anyone in his present state of mind; yet the boatswain had done well. Mr. MacMillan was a man to be watched—and in the best sense.

Back there a French frigate lay waiting to get in their whacks at this cheeky little English gun-boat. There was plenty of water in which to wear around and so go past in the darkness and pick up *Darter*. Fox was as Foxey as ever.

"Prepare to go about, Mr. Watson."

"Aye aye, sir." Then, with the hint of anxiety in his voice that Fox noted down in his mind, "We shall wear, of course, sir?"

"We will tack, Mr. Watson." Then, he added in the form, "If you please."

Now the men would know the kind of tearaway they had as their new commander. Instead of wearing around with the wind and so moving away from the shore and the frigate, he was going to tack, and so approach the shore and that damned great frigate. This was no time for heroics. This was a time to show these new men of his that in war only war-guts would do.

About to give the order, Fox paused. He stared ahead. Was that a darker smudge against the water, a blot of deeper darkness? He turned to Grey.

"What do you make of that, Mr. Grey?"

Grey looked. "Lay me horizontal, sir, if that ain't the Froggy schooners! Looks like two of 'em, sir, moored abreast."

"I thought so. Very well." He lifted his voice. "Mr. Blythe! Put a broadside into those Frog schooners as we

97

go past and after we have tacked kindly have the larboard broadside follow suit."

"Aye aye, sir."

Fox didn't care what anyone thought. He had no intention of attempting to cut out the schooners. He would obey his instructions if he ignored them and got *Darter* out. But Fox was always a man to exceed his instructions, and, anyway, those pesky schooners were the cause of this débacle.

Blythe let his carronades off in splendid style. They belched their flames and smoke and Fox saw the schooners wilt in the water. Then the business of tacking in confined waters occupied everyone's attention. "Helm's alee!" The tiller went over in grand style. *Minion* was caught at the precise moment she began to fall off. The foretacks and bowlines were hauled, *Minion* swung about onto her new course, heading straight back past the unhappy schooners. "Mr. Blythe!"

The eight carronades belched and thundered and the sorry schooners slumped even more. He might not wish to cut them out but, bigod, they certainly knew the navy had paid them a visit! They'd be hulks by now, if, that is, these confounded cack-handed gunners of his had shot straight. He made up his mind what he would do about that and the frigate, which was not a mere defenseless schooner with a copule of pop-gun four-pounders.

Minion straightened up on her reverse course. Now they were closer to the shore.

"By the mark five!" was followed on the next cast by: "By the deep four!" And that was followed by: "And a quarter less four!"

Yes, in those charts stored away in his head, yes, there was a spit here, a sandspit with the ominous figure one and a half writ large upon it.

"Ease her," he growled. And then, "Steady, steady." And then, as the leadsman called: "By the deep four!" Fox snarled: "Bring her back and hold her!"

"Aye aye, sir."

No thought of refusal to obey his orders in the wild confusion of the night action occurred to Fox, although the idea flashed across his mind's eye as a probability that had to be allowed for. He had a crew who were willing enough to try again, he saw that. They had had a rough time of it. Whatever else they might resent, they did not resent a man who knew what he was doing and handled himself resolutely and who scorned danger. For they knew, now, that Commander Fox was a man who did know what he was doing.

That thought made Fox change his mind about going down and personally sighting along every line of metal. He'd rather run the risk of missing the French than—in this new magnanimous paternal-commander role—of further inflaming this unknown crew by a clear display of his lack of confidence in them. Later on, of course, he'd let them see just how little he thought of their gunnery—if it was proved bad. Until then he was far more concerned over the safety of his command, of getting *Darter* out, and of not getting killed. These were the concerns of a man and would sound very strange in the ears of one of these fiery, cut-and-thrust, obnoxious French-hating officers so tiresomely familiar in the service.

The French frigate might survive to fight another day; but so would *Minion's* effectiveness as a fighting machine.

Minion heeled a little more as the breeze gusted. It blew straight across their larboard side. Fox became aware that he could make out Grey's face without the need of any reflected light. The French had stopped firing rockets. A greyness hung in the air.

Fox filled his lungs and bawled: "Make sure every shot hits! You'll be able to see the bastard when we get down with her."

Only an idiot would miss the corollory of that, that the French would be able to see them, too . . .

In the event the light from the east, misty and pallid like the belly of a shark, illuminated *Minion* far more than the frigate under the land. Visibility slowly increased as the brig swept down. Fox looked over the starboard beam. Yes, *Darter* was still there, creeping out with her sweeps going like a paralytic beetle and a scrap of canvas on her stunted mainmast. Grey had seen that the boatswain, Mr. MacMillan, had done a good job on the hawser. It would be necessary, there was no disguising that.

There was positive evil in letting the hands wait about like this as their vessel went down the inlet with her canvas pouting and her carronades run out and everyone tensed. Fox bawled orders that, whilst not strictly necessary, gave a further insurance for what might happen. The hawser was flexed out afresh, everything ready at the capstan, for *Minion* had been fitted with a capstan in preference to the windlass so often fitted into small craft, and the sail trimmers were employed to brace the yards to get the utmost from the breeze.

Fox peered through the pearly early moring mist off the water. He couldn't see the damn Frenchman. If anything the mist grew with the strengthening of the light.

That was to be expected. Maybe the Frogs wouldn't see them so easily, after all . . .

Then the frigate fired.

As soon as the first tongue of flame lashed out, scorching orange through the mist, Fox bellowed: "Open fire!"

The carronades began to bang off and the driver gaff

erupted in a shower of chips and whirled end over end like a monstrous barbarian caber to plunge into the sea trailing ripped vangs and ensign halliards and braces like a maniacal whaler's harpoon. A gunner screamed and clapped his brown hands to his face. Fox saw an eye dangling on its thread between his fingers. He roared the bosun into clearing the mess and then there was time only to yell amid the smoke and hoarsely encourage the men to reload in record time.

They still only got off two broadsides. The frigate fired a third that tore the sea to shreds well aft.

Watson, the master, began some remark to convey his relief.

Fox had observed the angle in the pattern of the last broadside. The gun flashes had been compacted, appearing closer together. Perspective must account for some of that tighter bunching—but not all . . .

"Prepare to take *Darter* in tow, if you please, Mr. Grey."

"Aye aye, sir."

They were coming down on the other gun-brig nicely now.

He must judge his exact moment when to order the topsails backed so as to take off enough way to make the task of getting the cable aboard that much easier. Fox, himself, would make the initial cast. It might be undignified in the captain of a vessel to descend to a menial task of this nature in person; but that was not only Fox's way, it was the way of the most professional of sea officers. If there was no one aboard who could do a certain task as efficiently as the captain, then it was the captain's task to assign that job to himself.

Fox swung the leadline with its weight around his head

well clear of the shrouds and the apparently mazelike rigging of *Minion*. *Darter's* stern crept past. Her men were pulling with a frenzied effort that betrayed the vehemence both of the colts upon their backs and their commanders' knowledge that to be caught in the Roulet by full daylight would be the end for them.

Fox took a look back. Yes, he thought so.

"Mr. Grey! Make it cheerly, now!"

"Aye aye, sir!"

"Mr. Watson. Kindly keep me informed of the progress of the frigate. I do not wish him to take us by surprise."

Watson spun about as though trapped on a precipice.

"The frigate, sir?" He looked back. "My God! She's coming out after us!"

"What did you expct, Mr. Watson, a visiting card first?"

Now he shouldn't have said that. That was the old Fox cutting into people who didn't think three steps ahead.

"Ahoy, *Darter!*" He roared it out with the full force of his lungs. "Prepare to receive a line!"

The answering hail reached him, shrill and excited.

He swung and as he swung so all his skill with the sling surged back, old days of hunting wildfowl on the Thames marshes impelling the skill of eye and brain and muscle. The line flew true. Someone aboard *Darter* secured it and at once the thicker line began to be paid out.

"Mr. Blythe!" Fox bellowed orders, and the topsails backed enough so that *Minion's* speed fell to match that of *Darter's* under sweeps. Fox judged distances and had no time to worry about his left eye's malfunctions. Grey had the hawser out now, being hauled across, and the boatswain was bellowing and striking about with his rattan. Whatever had gone wrong was quickly rectified and the hawser went on paying out.

102

Soon *Darter's* people had the hawser made fast.

Now Fox had to ease the strain on. Towing was a nasty little art, when you thought about it; he was in sheltered waters and that was a help, anyway. He looked back. The frigate now showed her three masts very close together and even as he looked so more canvas came out, gleaming pale, like watered silk, in that dawning light.

This smacked of two little lambs attempting to crawl away from the loping power of a wolf.

For the moment nothing more could be done.

"Mr. Grey! You have the deck."

To Grey's astonished "Aye aye, sir!" Fox jumped for the ladder way and clattered down. His tiny cabin looked poor and insignificant, and the central space was occupied by George Williams and William George, able seamen both, whom it had been the whim of the moment to assign to the task of handling the second tiller. Their names had given Fox a moment of sober hilarity, in his dour fashion. Life at sea demanded petty amusements at times.

He fetched out the atrocious chart of the Roulet. He knew he remembered; but it paid to double-check. He stood, his head bowed and shoulders hunched, brooding down on the chart spread out across his cot which had been unswung and stowed. There was no opportunity here to strike anything below; below was a single stuffed hold.

Yes, he said to himself, and his face took on the semblance of a devil's mask, so that Williams and George sucked in their breaths, their cheeks hollow, and laid their bronzed arms along the loom of the tiller, listening for the shouted words of command so that they might co-ordinate their movements with the timoneer on the upper tiller.

Yes, he'd trust that weird inner instinct of his for taking ships through shallow and treacherous waters. With a forty-four-gun frigate on his tail there was nothing else he could do. If he piled *Minion* up and *Darter*, with her lesser draught, collided, that would be the least of his worries, for the French frigate would, unless they surrendered, blow them both clean out of the water.

CHAPTER NINE

With the figures and the configurations indelibly imprinted on his mind, George Abercombie Fox went up on deck prepared to take on the frigate—and the rest of the damned French Navy, if needs be.

He oriented himself instantly, as was the way with any sea officer of any value, and assured himself that *Darter* still towed well, that the sails were set and pulling with the utmost efficiency and that the frigate had shaken out her courses and was following on track.

Fox cocked an eye up at the maintopsail. It slanted braced up to take full advantage of the breeze sweeping in over the larboard beam. He had lost his spanker gaff, and so the brig-rig, so handy under the hands of a man who understood the delicacy of balance, would become a nightmare to control. And there was *Darter* lurching at his stern and her pull had to be figured into the equations.

And—there was the matter of the strain on the hawser to consider. He couldn't just clap on all plain sail and get out of here as fast as he could. That way if he didn't snap the hawser he'd rip out the bitts, or bring down some vital spar, or do something horrible to *Darter*. He had to calculate to a nicety.

"Mr. Grey. I'll trouble you to set the royals."

"Aye aye, sir!"

Nothing else from Grey, no questions, no comment, nothing beyond that regulation 'aye aye, sir.' Well, Gray could say nothing else, of course; but Fox did not miss the sudden instinctive forward movement of the master. Mr. Watson jerked, and then stopped, as though smitten by the Gorgons.

The hands clambered aloft smartly enough. There was some hitch about the fore royal; but at last the canvas came tumbling down and could be sheeted home and the yard braced around. Fox caught a little more at the feel of *Minion*. The men were eager to please. There was no doubt about that. But, always, it seemed, in the midst of their endeavors something would go wrong.

"Mr. Grey. Would you kindly ascertain why the fore royal was set by loblolly boys? Or was the captain of the foretop having a caulk? Or, perhaps, the foretopmen would care to be rated waisters?"

Grey cocked that impassive but mocking eye on his captain. Fox didn't give a damn what young Grey might think.

"Aye aye, sir," said Grey, and took himself off.

"The Frog is fair foaming along, sir, said Watson.

Fox did not look back over the unhappy and laborious hulk of *Darter*.

"So I expect, Mr. Watson."

He took a turn up and down that ridiculous quarterdeck.

"Mr. Watson. You will know. I want the best leadsman in this vessel in the chains. And, Mr. Watson, I shall require the utmost expedition in compliance with my orders. We are going to do that Frog's business for him before he does ours."

"Aye aye, sir—that'll be Rosen, sir. He volunteered out of an East Indiaman. I think there was some trouble—"

Fox did not grunt or make that silly ha-harrumph so many captains were slaves to. "If he volunteered, Mr. Watson, you may bet your life's savings there was trouble."

That was the way. Let the merchant ships train up prime seamen, and then let the Navy take them, by impressment or volunteering, anyway, so that the muscles of England were powered by professionals as well as the arteries.

G. A. Fox took another turn up and down. He rather cared for that image. Perhaps Wordly might have done something more with it. Muscles of the navy and arteries of the merchantmen. Yes. Apt, that—

A sullen boom from aft made Fox turn, at last, to look back.

The frigate had fired one of her bow chasers. *Darter* was going to take punishment before this little business was through.

Fox puckered up his lips. He was going to need more maneuverability from his horrible little vessel than the square canvas would give him. He passed the word for the boatswain, the carpenter and the sailmaker to lay aft.

"Anything that will draw will do. A kind of staysail. From the maintop. Cut up the driver. Just get on with the work and never mind anybody else. Mr. MacMillan—not you. I shall need you from time to time."

"Aye aye, sir," said MacMillan.

The sailmaker screwed up his eyes in a gesture of deep

thought. "I reckon as how it c'd be done, sir. Aye, for my part I'll give you a sail that'll draw prime, sir."

"Very good."

The carpenter, Mr. Shayne, nodded with a briskness Fox felt to be genuine. "I'll get the remains o' the gaff cleared away, sir. The jaws and parral and six foot o' gaff is still there to foul the work."

He spoke like a professional expounding, as though unaware that the mess he was talking about was not hanging above their heads in full view.

"Very good," said Fox again. It was always a pleasure to talk to standing officers, and to delve with them into the arcane mysteries of their lore. More than one crusty old warrant officer with thirty years sea experience had been astonished that Mr. Fox could tell him things about ships he'd never even dreamed existed. Now Commander Fox would not forgo that pleasure.

When the little group broke up and the warrant officers took themselves off to bellow their yeomen and their crews into action on their specialities, Fox took considerable pleasure, also, that not once had one of the men so much as stared aft where the menacing shape of the frigate pursued them. The light misted over for a space and then, miraculously, cleared and it was day.

The necessary routine of the vessel carried on and Fox spent his time staring at the land to larboard as it trended in towards their course, narrowing the Roulet. Down there lay the Petit Mallou. No sounds came from there. Either the British had taken it or they hadn't. Either way the French would have the advantage. If the British had failed to storm the battery then the thirty-six-pounders would simply tear the two gun-boats to pieces. If the fort had been taken the French could calmly wait to see if the maniac in command of the gun-boat towing the other would attempt to take off the marines and seamen, or cover their boats, or ignore them. Either way, as Fox saw it from the French point of view, the French must think they held a winning hand—with that damn great frigate pounding up astern.

He just hoped *Darter* was not taking too much punishment.

"Put the leadsman—Rosen, isn't it—into the chains, now, if you please."

Mr. Watson, as the master, would deal with that. Fox let his eyes take in the view beginning from the land to larboard ahead, right around to starboard, to broad on the beam where the opposite shoreline showed plainly, a low streak against the early-morning glitter of the water and the high pale sky, right around past the quarter, to dead astern. The wind tended to shift *Darter* out a little; but Fox was not concerned with that, for *Darter* drew eighteen inches less than *Minion*. The tide wouldn't help, for the fouling of the plan which had accounted for the flood going in and the ebb coming out meant they were on a falling tide now.

He swung his gaze over *Darter*, past the ominous shape following which, even as he looked, emitted a puff of smoke. The bang followed thereafter. Even by a close observation of *Darter*, Fox could not see if the shot struck. Once that frigate drew abreast of them she'd pound *Darter* into wreckage and then move onto her consort. If Fox let her, of course.

He swung his gaze forward along the coastline, which really looked rather dull and uninteresting, and so forward again off the larboard bow. They had to negotiate the pool and the bend, and the Petit Mallou was coming up. Fox conjured the charts in his mind's eye.

The French captain would almost certainly have better

charts, more modern ones. He would not blindly follow Fox onto a sandbank . . . But Fox was not a Foxey fellow for nothing.

Going back to the timoneer he stood, his hands tucked up behind his back, his head jutting forward with that abominable old hat of his a monstrosity under the sun. He had clapped it on for this night's work in preference to the fancy new hats he had bought when appointed first of *Hector*, with the loan from Staunton, which had all been repaid. Now, with that old hat with its saber cut square on his head, he felt he could get down to business. The helmsman fully aware of his captain's stare upon him kept stolidly to his task, feeling the brig along as the flukey wind played with his control.

"You'll soon have a bastard-driver, Kellet," said Fox. "Then you'll find she'll answer more handily."

"Aye aye, sir."

"I shall be requiring instant attention from you, Kellet. I'm told you're a first class hand. We'll find out."

"Aye aye, sir, thank'ee, sir."

"Because, Kellet, if you fail me we'll end up on a mudbank, and we'll either rot in a French gaol or we'll be fishbait."

Kellet's bronzed throat jumped as he swallowed, and then he said sturdily: "Aye aye, sir."

Then Fox gave the orders that would start the farce in train.

He felt it to be a farce—here he was, with a lubberly gun-boat, with a crippled vessel in tow, attempting to outfight a smart French forty-four. Bigod! If he brought this one off they ought to allow him to shift his swab from his left shoulder to his right!

The orders took care of all the extraneous things necessary. Since *Minion* had been cleared for action and the men at battle stations from the beginning of the action—if this night's affair could be so grandiloquently styled—makeshift arrangements had to be undertaken to feed the hands. The hammocks remained in their cranes. *Minion* edged shorewards.

Because of the wind pressure, even at sea level, *Darter* hung a little into the offing from *Minion*. The Frenchman kept outside *Darter*. He was fairly clipping along now and although Fox's calculations told him he'd get to his aiming point before the frigate could range up alongside, it would be nip and tuck.

The French frigate's sails curved beautifully in the morning breeze. Her forefoot rode with scarcely a plunge, sending a long streaming wake aft. She looked a beauty. Again that puff of smoke broke over her beakhead and this time Fox saw the shot plunge into the sea off *Darter's* larboard quarter. The seconds ticked away. *Minion* edged nearer and the land broadened and the Petit Mallou dominating the bend in the Roulet approached. There was a little village on the opposite shore, and no doubt the people were up and about early all agog with the doings in the inlet. The bend was going to be tricky. It seemed perfectly obvious to Fox that the French frigate captain knew he must catch the British before that; equally, it must be clear to him that the wind would be dead foul for them all, if the flukey airs did not shift by a good few points.

With the two being hauled along like a recalcitrant horse by its bridle, *Minion* was kept on her own course as to direction; she tended to yaw violently every now and then and Kellet and his mate had to sweat over their tiller and the cry would go down to the two below, Williams and George, to co-operate.

The sailmaker in a vast ripping was refashioning the

driver. He had not suggested they should use the ringtail. Fox agreed. The ringtail was designed to act as a species of stunsail rigged on booms extending outwards from the gaff and the boom, and its shape would be both too narrow in the foot and too broad elsewhere. Fox kept his two eyes—which were both operating beautifully—everywhere observing what was going on, inboard, over the side and also in *Darter*. She had continued to use her sweeps, and the consequent jerking on the hawser did not please Fox; but for the moment he wanted as much speed as he could get. If it all went smash then he would have miscalculated.

The chart stood in the forefront of his brain. He could see every marking and indentation as though it hung in the air before his eyes. The tide was on the ebb. The bend and the island up ahead approached. The light strengthened and as it did so Fox felt the shift in the breeze. The flukey airs were backing. He felt confident of that. That would give the Frenchman a nasty thought or two, for the wind, if it continued to back, would no longer be dead foul for the British to make their escape down the Roulet.

"What do you make of the island, Mr. Grey?"

Grey took the big telescope from its beckets and sprang up onto the ratlines. He balanced easily, a youthful, lithe figure, debonair and handsome, and Fox in his own ugly way stared deliberately away back at *Darter*.

"Can't make the colors out, sir. It looks like the Union —yes, I'm sure it is—yes, sir—it's the Union!"

"Very good, Mr. Grey."

So there was one problem solved. The marines and the seamen there would be piling down into their boats ready to pull out to safety. What they would make of this hairy great frigate breathing down their protectors' necks Fox wouldn't care to hazard a guess. Everything had happened

112

with an incredible slowness, and yet the time had in reality flickered by at top speed.

Mr. Watson was fidgeting again.

Mr. Grey had not jumped down off the ratlines. He kept his telescope trained forward over the larboard beam. Fox knew all about that. He knew what Grey was saying.

He supposed he would have to put them out of their misery of anticipation and plunge them into a turmoil of conjecture. They would know he was a maniac now, for sure.

"Mr. Watson." Fox spoke it out, harshly, in his goddam-you-to-hell voice. "I shall take *Minion* through on the shoreside of the Petit Mallou."

CHAPTER TEN

Naval discipline held Mr. Watson for a heartbeat. Then his fidgeting burst out.

"The shoreside, sir! But that is practically dry at low water!"

Fox did not look at him.

He had more than half expected this. Watson was a good master, he felt from what he had seen of him; but he fussed. The idea of hazarding his ship filled him with the kind of horror a gaggle of nuns in an Italian seminary must feel when Bonaparte's atheistic grenadiers burst in.

Grey jumped down from the ratlines and took remarkably few strides across the deck to stand before the master. What Grey said Fox did not hear; but shortly thereafter Watson walked back to the binnacle and remained, his face set and stiff, as though dipped in starch.

At any potential court martial that might subsequently be held Watson would surely be able to uphold and substantiate any disobedience of that order. Fox didn't intend to give him the chance to disobey—and then he realized that Grey had done all that for him. He'd trained young Grey up well, it seemed, in the time they'd served together.

Someone was waving from *Darter's* bows. He could guess what that was all about. He ignored that, as he ignored the thin yells that drifted past. Grey took a turn up and down and looked at Watson, and no one dared to call their captain's attention to the hails from the tow.

Minion was now well over to the larboard shore, and the breeze had backed with immense consideration so that the wind now blew over their larboard quarter and the sail trimmers were bracing the yards ever more squarely across the deck. Fox walked back to Kellet and Mr. Watson moved out of his way.

Fox spoke to the master as though nothing had passed between them of any nature other than subjects of strict professional competence.

"If you'll kindly begin heaving the lead, Mr. Watson, I shall be much obliged."

"Aye aye, sir."

At the first cast Rosen in the chains yelled: "By the mark seven!" That meant he had a red bunting marker between his fingers. Forty-two feet of water was to be expected here where the current would scour the bottom before swirling around the island and widening into that shallow pool outside. Inside, the bottom would shelve and shelve until at exceptional tides when the moon was new or full the sand would glisten ominously through a few inches of water. The almanack was being kind to George Abercrombie Fox. It was a day past the first quarter, and apart from an unexpected act of God an honest sailorman could expect a neap tide, when the rise and fall is at minimum.

Now it must be clear to even the dullest head that the

115

lunatic English captain was attempting to take his vessel, with another in tow, past on the inside of the Petit Mallou. They must be cursing and steaming over on the island. The Frenchman must be mon dieuing and sacre bleuing away, and no doubt slapping his thigh in great good humor that he had a madman to deal with.

"By the deep six!"

Fox spoke quite gently to Kellet and the seaman eased the tiller more, so that *Minion* set herself squarely for the jaws of the island and the spit off from the mainland. *Darter* still hung a little to leeward; but with the shift of the wind and the closeness of the shore the breeze passed more above her with only that stump of a mainmast left. She began to line up exactly astern of *Minion*.

Then they were into the trap with a vengeance.

"By mark three!"

They had reached into shoal water with savage suddenness.

"And a quarter less three!"

Fox wasn't worried about *Darter*. She drew a good eighteen inches less, and where *Minion* could go *Darter* could follow.

"By the mark two!"

Well, he was in for it, now.

The island passed on their starboard. It looked a featureless platelike excrescence rising from the water, with a few scrubby bushes and the dark bulk of the fort just visible on the opposite side. Now all could see the Union flying from the staff over there.

"Marines, sir!"

Fox could see them, trotting across the sand and mud. Now why the devil hadn't they got into their boats? The scarlet tunics blazed in the early sun, bayonets all atwinkle.

116

Then Fox saw a gaggle of boats creeping out from the island and the marines jog-trotting to reach them. In the instant that the marines reached the boats and began to clamber aboard a vast explosion tore upwards from the fort. Fort, battery, flag, everything went skywards in a blossom of flame and a geyser of smoke. A toadstool top formed and billowed and spread.

The wind scattering burning debris away downwind, but the shock wave drove *Minion* shuddering sideways, and the yell of the leadsman was lost.

This Rosen was a man who knew his job, for even as the silence dropped ringing about everyone's ears, he called out high and shrill: "And a quarter less two!"

Fox heard Grey say: "It'll be damned close!"

No time to humor Mr. Lionel Grey . . . Time to stare back at the French frigate and see if the Frog was doing what he ought to do—yes! The three masts with their press of canvas opened out as he hauled away from the fierce direct pursuit. He was going through the channel, around the outside of the Petit Mallou, driving his ship where sane people sailed . . .

No doubt the Frenchman had been thinking with some Gallic joviality when he saw the gun-boats heading into shoal water that the mad Englishman expected him to follow meekly and rip his bottom out or stick fast. And then, this jovial Frenchman would have thought, chuckling, he would do no such thing. He would simply continue his course in deep water and range up alongside the pair of gun boats and shatter them with his broadside. That was what Fox would have done, what any competent seaman would have done. The Frenchman had a new twist to cope with now, and Fox wished him well of it.

"And a quarter less two!"

The bottom was keeping level, then . . .

The frigate had farther to go, around the outside of the island. The British boats were all away now, heading down the inlet and angling to come alongside the gunboats. Fox looked forrard again, his thin lips compressed. He was not about to humor a flock of gigs and cutters, not now, not even if Mr. Midshipman Gruber and his marines were in them.

"By the mark two!"

Watson could not restrain himself. "By God! We're over!"

Fox felt it politic to let Watson know what real kind of black bastard he had found in his new captain.

"I think not, Mr. Watson." His voice lifted. "Mr. Grey. Kindly oblige me by having the fo'c'sle men lay aft. Cheerly now!"

"Aye aye, sir."

The rush of naked feet on the deck and the hoarse grunts as the seamen pounded aft made Fox rap out: "Silence, all of you, and keep out of my way. Back to the taffrail and give the tiller a wide berth!"

The hands clustered right aft. Now that damned hanging forefoot of his ought to balance out. *Minion* should, if his calculations were reasonable as he felt they were, ride evenly through the water.

"By the mark two!"

Over the flat slab of the island the three masts of the frigate were going along with a smooth stateliness in their progression that filled Fox with both envy and desire—desire to knock them down, all three. The Frenchman was taking his ship down the Roulet in good order, all ready to resume the chase when the idiotic English reappeared from the far end of the shallow channel between island and shore.

The boats were now broad on the beam.

118

They'd have to be towed out. The ebb was running now and that would assist them; but the men would be exhausted after a night's strenuous effort, of fighting and storming the fort. There would be wounded.

"And a quarter less two!"

Now for it.

Now they were running across the stretch ominously pocked by those figures of one and a half. Fox half-turned to face the hands clustered by the taffrail.

"Get ready to run forrard—and I mean *run!* When I give the word I want you up on th fo'c'sle as though a bailiff was on your heels."

One or two essayed a guffaw at this, instantly stilled.

Minion rode level. Fox said: "I want twenty more bodies to lay aft, Mr. Grey. Kindly sort 'em out."

Grey would pick the men who were nimble enough to leap along a cumbered deck, avoiding ropes and lines, leaping tackle, men agile enough to do what Fox required. Fox knew Grey would know what men to select, for Fox knew that Grey understood the situation, and, as a good first lieutenant, had made himself master of his men in short order. Fox had done it many times; he saw no reason why Grey should not.

The twenty lay aft and now *Minion* rode stern deep.

"And a quarter less two!"

A quiet word to Kellet brought the head around a fraction to starboard. The short cut behind the island meant that *Minion* had much less distance to go than the frigate. Fox made no move to take off any canvas.

"And a quarter less two!"

"Starboard your helm, midships, steady," and Fox kept *Minion's* bowsprit fixed on his aiming mark.

He looked again across the starboard quarter. The frigate was now clearly astern of them, still going along with

119

her canvas drawing beautifully; but her wide sweep around the Petit Mallou meant she would be well astern when they came out the far end of the short cut channel. Fox did not smile; but he felt a great joy possess him.

He had left Sophy—and had once more embraced the sea and ships, and he wouldn't miss this excursion for the world.

"And a half less two!"

Instantly Fox rapped his orders. Grey and the boatswain were ready.

"Let go the hawser!"

Men sprang to obey and the hawser fell clear to splash into the wake, even as Rosen in the chains sang out: "And a half less two!"

In that exact second, *Minion* struck.

She shuddered. Fox heard the groan torn from her fabric, and he heard the high keening of her rigging.

"Forrard!" roared Fox. "Forrard or I'll have the hides off you!"

The hands clustered at the taffrail ran like a herd of panicking sheep, racing forward along the deck. Heaven was on Fox's side, for the sticks had not been ripped out of her. As the weight was transferred forward so *Minion's* forefoot would go down in the water. But because her stern had been down when she struck her keel had met sand about amidships. Now she tilted forward, rocking on her center of balance. The breeze gusted and with a lurching and a queasy sucking she slid forward and was free.

"*Darter's* signalling, sir," said Watson.

"Not now, Mr. Watson."

Minion rode forward, and aft the water boiled and writhed with disturbed sand yellow and golden and thick beneath the surface.

"By the deep four!"

"This time," said Grey. "This time, for sure!"

Grey cast a look at his captain, and then took a pace forward and bellowed a fiercely intemperate order for the hands to resume their battle stations. Fox looked up at the set of his yards, at his tacks, and then back and at the frigate.

"We have the bastard, Mr. Grey! By God, we have him!"

"I am most happy to say I agree with you, sir."

Fox could tolerate this from Grey; they were apparently merely expressing the familiar sentiments of British naval officers about to go into action; but Fox knew that between him and Grey there was more, and Grey underlined those feelings by adding: "Lay me horizontal, sir; but I'll wager Mr. Carker would give a deal to be here, and I'd be damned glad to see him."

This was highly magnanimous of Grey!

Fox stared at his first lieutenant from those ice-cold chips of eyes, and said: "I'm glad to hear it, Mr. Grey. For Mr. Carker would be senior to you, I believe."

"Aye, sir—but—but, goddammit! I'd still like to see him here!"

You couldn't say more than that.

"And a half four!"

"Very good," said Fox. He glared forward. The ship's boy who had stood so silently all during these moments of tension and on whose narrow shoulders rested the responsibility of acting as captain's messenger jumped as Fox spoke to him.

"Run to Mr. Blythe, lad. My compliments, and will he pray step onto the quarterdeck."

"Aye aye, sir," squeaked the little mouse-voice and the lad hared off.

Here came the boatswain and the sailmaker. They

looked pleased. All the period when *Minion* ran over the shallows and the hands had been steeple-chasing up and down the deck they had had their crews hard at work overhead.

"Juryrig all ready for inspection, sir."

"Very good, Mr. MacMillan. We'll have this vessel behaving as she should in short order."

Blythe approached, touching his hat.

"Now, Mr. Blythe." Fox spoke briskly, all the no-nonsense captain. "We are going to cross that Frenchman's bows .and we will rake her. Mr. Blythe. I want every carronade in the starboard battery to fire. I want every carronade doubled shotted with grape stuffed down on top. Mr. Blythe, I want every carronade to hit. Is that understood?"

"Aye aye, sir."

"Yes, Mr. Blythe, aye aye, sir, it is. But is it understood?"

"Aye aye, sir—Understood, sir."

"Very good. Now, I want the six-pounder to fire at the Frog's topmasts. Use chain-shot. I would dearly like to be able to put in my report that Lieutenant Blythe's excellent control of the gun battery resulted in that bloody frigate's foretopmast coming down. Am I understood, again, Mr. Blythe?"

"Blythe swallowed. "Aye aye, sir. Understood, sir."

"Make it so."

Blythe took himself off, and Fox made sure he had a good long look from time to time, as *Minion* rounded the end of the Petit Mallou, along the gundeck. Blythe was going around to every carronade and what he was saying brought a stiffness into the backs of the men, and an alacrity in their work.

Fox didn't smile often; he didn't smile now; but a slight rictus about his thin lips might have been observed.

"By the deep six!"

This would be the scoured tailings of the channel. The frigate now showed her masts over the starboard quarter. *Minion* in her desperate dash through the shallows had gained a long lead. Fox glanced up. He ought to shorten sail right now and on the instant gave the order and the topmen poured aloft to take in the royals. Fox wasn't one of your die-hard old shellbacks who would never set their royals for fear of carrying something away and incurring the wrath of dockyard and admiral; but in confined waters like this handiness was the vital factor.

The frigate's three masts were growing closer and closer together, appearing to sprout from the island, her hull hidden.

One of the more interesting aspects of these fascinating calculations that absorbed George Abercrombie Fox as he took a turn up and down his ridiculous little quarterdeck with his blue uniform coat rather shabby in the brightening sun and his white trousers grubby about the knees and full of wrinkles, had to do with the rapidity of comprehension of the French captain in the frigate. The fellow might be a clever sea officer, or a dunderhead pushed up by the Revolution and a few rolling heads in the baskets. Either way, he was pressing on under all plain sail with his driver and jib giving him balance, and he showed no inclination to halt that frenzied onward rush.

Fox came to the tentative conclusion that the Frenchman had, in observing how the English gunboats had drawn ahead of him, determined to catch them up.

Mind you, his charts would show the latest channel scoured in the Roulet. The wide pool outside of the Petit Mallou would be too shallow for the frigate although enough for *Minion*. But—Monsieur Crapaud might have an ace tucked somewhere up his Revolutionary sleeve . . .

A look aloft showed Fox his bastard-driver working well, curving boldly in a sheer triangular wedge from the maintop to the spanker boom. The thing *was* working well; Fox could tell that from the feel of his vessel. Maybe a gaff wasn't so all-fired necessary, after all . . . Then the foolishness of that kind of thought took him, remembering all the outlandish kinds of rigs there were ploughing the Mediterranean, or up in the Baltic, come to that, and he put it from his mind, except to allow a little pleasure that he'd stuck to his fore and aft mainsail, although thus cut down to a bastard-driver, in preference to his square mainsail. The breeze was going to continue flukey all day.

As the angles subtended so Fox felt the presentiment of the coming action like the flicker of distant lightning of a summer storm. If his calculations worked out correctly—hell! There was no if aboat it! They *were* going to work out correctly—then his command should lambast the Frog with little chance of any return fire coming in. The bowchasers might spit and bang; the English would ignore that.

Grey had been pacing some, at least, of his captain's thoughts, for he sang out: "He's taking his royals in, sir!"

"Aye, the devil take him!"

The French frigate was coming around the bend outside the Petit Mallou, pent into the deep-water channel. From his larboard side and out of the mouth of the narrow gut between island and shore the English gunboat was now swinging to emerge square across his bows. He could not turn aside. He could take his way off only slowly short of throwing out an anchor, which would dismast him in a trice. Now Fox had he been of that kidney could have gloated. The Frog was hurtling helplessly down into disaster.

124

For the benefit of Watson, and wilting a little at what Mr. Grey might think, Fox said: "If I commanded the frigate I'd bear straight on and ram us."

"Drastic, sir," observed Grey, coolly. "But safest."

Watson licked his lips. Then, lifting his head, he said: "I agree, sir. That would be the wisest course."

Even then Fox wasn't prepared to bet that Watson did fully agree. It would be hazarding his ship, and that Watson was not prepared to do, or so surmised Fox, the cynical.

The sure onward progress of the two vessels resembled some ritual dance. The frigate coming down the inlet, the gun-boat swinging out across her bows with all that wide if shallow pool in which to maneuver, both were held in lines of force originating and directed in the minds of their captains.

"Stand to your guns!" Blythe was bellowing.

The men were already there, in position, keyed-up. Blythe wanted to do well. Fox felt he could look to Blythe in the future as an officer on whom, if he oversaw just what it was he was doing, he might rely.

The gun-boat left the last tailing of the island. Rosen came out of the chains. For a leadsman he was relatively dry, his clothes spattered rather than drenched. Grey was up in the ratlines again, shading his eyes, staring at the frigate which now, with her three masts almost in line, became visible from cutwater to truck. She still looked an incredibly beautiful sight, with her canvas curved and proud, the sun glinting off her, her flags fluttering, the white water breaking and swirling back from her forefoot.

Fox judged the subtended angles. He had managed it just right. As *Minion* re-entered the main channel of the inlet, going across, she presented all her broadside to the Frenchman. The carronades would reach that distance

125

with no trouble at all. Fox looked along his deck. His own deck, his men, his crew, his officers. He took off that battered atrocity of a hat, lifting it, waving it in the air.

"As your guns bear!" he roared. *"Open fire!"*

CHAPTER ELEVEN

Flame and smoke jetted from *Minion's* side.

The six-pounder fired first. Fox had an especial interest in the performance of that gun. As the carronades smashed their enormous roars into the morning daylight and the brown smoke gushed up, recoiling and billowing as it met the breeze, Fox watched the beautiful pile of canvas over there that drove the French frigate along so splendidly.

Nothing—nothing—yes!

By God!

Yes!

The foretopgallant mast swayed. Lines snapped. Then the mast and yard and sail crumpled and fell all smash down and the foretopmast in its turn buckled and with yard and sail wrapped like old sacking pitched overside.

The men set up a shrill cheering. Fox let them get on with it, for he saw the galvanic form of Mr. Blythe energetically urging them on. Fox had noted how keyed up the men had been, and had like any good commander not relished that. They should have been alert and yet relaxed, not under tension, ready to give their best in fighting their carronades. But Blythe and the gun-crews between them had done the job. Smoke blew back and Fox could see the head of the frigate hideously disfigured, scarred, with splintered scantlings starkly upthrown, the spritsail a wreck, the whole front of the ship savagely marked.

She might be a tiny and lubberly brig, might *Minion*, but at this range she had mighty big teeth!

Now they were past, heading into the shallow pool, and the island and the frigate were falling away astern. Fox wanted plenty of room to come around. He looked back. The activity on the deck of the frigate, heads bobbing, men racing up the shrouds of the foremast, told him she was nowhere near beaten yet. But he'd raked her. He'd raked her for and aft with eight massive thirty-two-pounders, double-shotted and loaded with grape. She would be a shambles on the tween decks.

Men were scampering aloft up the mainmast shrouds, also, as the angles widened and she came more broadside on, her masts opening out. She had fired her bowchasers; where the shot had gone Fox had no idea. Her maintopgallant sail came in, and then her maintopsail. Her way was coming off. Fox looked past her, at the shore. He pondered.

Those indelible lines of the chart stood brilliantly forth in his mind, hanging like mene mene tekel upharsin against his eyes.

Yes! The cunning bastard!

If Fox tacked around now and came back to pour in his larboard broadside he'd be running straight onto a spit of land . . . They'd skirted that as they pulled up here. Fox let his thin lips rick back.

"Prepare to go about. Mr. Watson, we will wear ship."

"Wear ship, aye aye, sir."

128

He'd go away to leeward with his shallow draught and flat bottom like that rice pudding on ice; but he'd avoid the sand pit.

Trapped as she was in the deep-water channel the frigate could either go on or stop. Fox fancied that if she took all her way off she could turn in the channel with her boats pulling head and tail. But if the Frenchman did that to bring his broadsides to bear, he would never stop the English. They would simply sail away. To a man like Fox no stupid notions of running would enter his mind. He wasn't shy; not like that bastard Lord Lymm. Now if Fox had had *Minion* under his command that time *Duchess* with Charles Beckworth, afterwards Lord Lymm, as the first lieutenant had so cravenly dived below and then brazened it out afterwards, that chasse maree would never have escaped. All Fox's searing contempt for the incompetents among his superiors aroused in him those old familiar sensations of never putting a foot wrong if he could help it, of doing what had to be done exactly right so as to bring about the desired resuḷ. And Fox's ways of doing things were very often so outrageous that had he had any friends in the navy they must have shuddered for his neck. But—weren't Carker and Grey friends? Were they? How could a foul-tempered, cynical, tarpaulin sea-officer believe that a bright young sprig like Grey or a sober conscientious officer like Carker could have any time for him at all? But, he felt with a bowel-stirring unease, bigod, they did. And the Frenchman was still coming on and it was time to haul *Minion* around again so as to get a crack in with her larboard broadside.

"Stand to your gun!"

The men moved with an alacrity that pleased Fox. They were still too keyed-up, too tense—this wasn't as though they faced the dangers of a general action or a single-ship duel in the open sea—and maybe this tightness of response to orders, this desire to please their new commander in fear of what had been happening aboard, lay at the root of the problem.

"There's something mighty funny going on on the Petit Mallou, sir," said Grey. He took the telescope from his eye and stared down at Fox from the ratlines. "Deuced odd, sir."

Minion was now curving sweetly back to get in her whacks at the frigate, which although still coming on had sensibly diminished her rush through the water. There was just time.

Fox leaped up into the ratlines and hung onto a shroud with his left hand, took the telescope from Grey and, under his first lieutenant's guidance, picked out what was going on on the island.

He looked for longer than he had intended, the circle of the telescope clear and bright, bringing out the details of the wrecked fort in startling clarity. A little smoke still hung over the scene of the explosion. But there were the dark energetic figures of men swarming around the banked casemates, swathes of debris leading away and onto the streaks of sand and mud. He saw a group concentrated onto some immense effort and held the telescope steady against the movement of his vessel.

Bigod!

Yes—so many foul abuses and blasphemies and general vile commentaries on commanders who could not do a simple job properly flooded into his mind he had to lock his jaws to prevent himself making a spectacle of himself, there in the shrouds of his own command.

They were French soldiers over there, and they were doing what French artillerymen would do, if given half the chance by some bungling incompetent of a British officer, with gold lace and a noble title and no brains.

He leaped down from the ratlines. He was bawling orders at the top of his voice.

The men responded as though the cat o' nine tails already licked hungrily across their naked backs.

Minion swung away from her careful course beyond the sand spit and away from the frigate. That larboard broadside now gaped shorewards. The French had seen his movement and he could imagine the swearing going on over there right now. There was no time for niceties now.

"Mr. Blythe! You have the range! Blow that bloody great gun into pieces before they—"

The thirty-six-pounder on the Petit Mallou fired.

Now the luck that had been with Fox deserted him.

A whirling mass of iron, an expanding shot, scythed through his riggings. Lines parted, the foretopgallant mast erupted into splinters, the jib collapsed, canvas and ropes and blocks cascaded down. Men screamed as the debris punched into them. Fox screamed for MacMillan to clear the raffle away.

Then Blythe fired and the carronades belched. The smoke blew only fitfully away and before it fully cleared another awful smash sounded aloft. More blocks spattered down. *Minion* was being hit by a master gunner over there.

The French captain of the frigate had brought his command down with no foretopmast—and although the Frog had three masts to play with, Fox would take his command out as well and be damned to him!

The smoke blew to leeward and Fox looked instantly to where the frigate lay up the inlet. She was turning! She had her boats out towing and from head and tail they exerted their pulls and were swinging her. Perhaps her bowsprit might overhang the shallows on one side and her jack those on the other; but she would have all her teeth exposed and ready along her broadside to rend and tear and destroy *Minion*!

"Out sweeps!" yelled Fox.

He had to do everything he could, now. They were still drifting down on the ebb. "Bos'n! Get that raffle cleared away now!"

Grey—without orders—went leaping forward with an axe swinging and plunged into the desperate task of hacking the wreckage away. *Minion* was easing forward. Her stern was showing to the Frenchman. Still he hadn't fired. Fox roared the hands on as the sweeps were hastily unshipped from stowage and thrust through the oar ports. He yelled at Kellet.

"Hard over, Kellet. Bring her larboard around."

They were swinging now as the sweeps bit. The breeze helped. They were swinging back as Kellet and his mates leaned on the tillers. Blythe was frantically urging his gun-crews on to reload in a time they had never bettered before. The starboard—unfired—battery now began to open out onto the frigate. They were almost around. Fox stared back with dancing anxiety—with as close as he would come to sheer panic—and he thought they would do it—and the Frenchman fired.

Chaos struck the gun-brig. Her light scantlings were battered and splintered by the blast. But, as usual, even on an even keel, the French had fired high. Men fell about the English vessel's decks as splinters and debris from above rained down on them; not one was struck by a roundshot or a parcel of grape.

Then—

"Fire!"

The Frog was firing twenty-four-pounders, and although he had more weapons than *Minion*, *Minion* was firing thirty-two-pounders. Fox, through the smoke, could see the havoc those massive guns were causing.

Then the next two thirty-sixes from the shore came in and, this time, only one struck, to add to the destruction aboard.

"Keep your rhythm!" yelled Fox. "Get those sweeps in and pull, you blagskites, *pull!*"

Minion turned and began to creep away. Now she could put her larboard broadside into the remains of a fort where six thirty-six-pounders had ostensibly been spiked by a party of British seamen and marines. The two thirty-sixes fired again and this time both missed. Fox looked back. His left eye had lost all vision some time ago, being completely closed off by that hateful ring of purple and black—but he had no idea when that had happened.

In the midst of danger when his head might be taken off by a roundshot at any minute or a charge of grape might punch his belly through his backbone, Fox took a deal of comfort from the realization that he had been fighting and functioning with his damned left eye completely closed off and had ridden over that handicap, had not noticed it; but had gone on roaring and battling as though nothing afflicted him.

The raffle of wreckage cumbering the decks was being sorted out by Grey and the boatswain and those of the hands not occupied at the sweeps and the carronades. Chunks of spars, blocks, lines all tangled, tattered canvas, all went over the side. And, going over also with the wreckage went the mangled bodies of men . . .

Fox looked back.

The Frenchman could outrange them, no doubt about that. But his next broadside resulted in only one hit, a splintering of chips and deadly whirring wooden spears fountaining up from the taffrail. Kellet ducked instinctively. Fox bellowed and Kellet straightened up, gripping the tiller. The Williams and the George were relieved from the second tiller and pitched in with the rest of the hands to make *Minion* something like a fighting vessel once more. Back from them and now just venturing into view from the shoreside of the Petit Mallou came *Darter*. Her people would have been able to read what had been happening from the changes in position of the masts of the combatants and the clouds of smoke. The boats pulled out also, and in an untidy procession headed down the inlet. Fox frowned. His ideas had been undergoing some considerable change in the last few minutes.

"Port your helm," he said.

He spoke firmly. He spoke matter-of-factly. But the moment the tiller was put over at his order and *Minion's* head began to turn to starboard everyone aboard knew that this maniac new commander of theirs was up to another harebrained scheme.

Fox waited as *Minion* turned and under her sweeps began to pull out from the deep-water channel. He waited, having decided to give Mr. Watson fifteen seconds.

At twelve Mr. Watson in his fussy way said: "Do you wish me to put a leadsman in the chains, sir?"

"I'd be obliged, Mr. Watson. Not Rosen. He's done his stint."

"Aye aye, sir." Watson perked up. Maybe that was the way to handle him, and probably it was; but in moments of stress and immediate danger Fox couldn't afford to wait around too long.

The leadsman's calls began and formed a continuing background to the action. The bottom remained fairly constant at around two and a half fathoms, and here Min-

134

ion could sail comfortably whilst the French frigate would ground.

The people in *Minion* were still reacting to orders with that willingness to jump that, Fox more and more suspected, stemmed from fear of what had happened, fear of what this new captain might do, fear of fear itself. This must have been the kind of command that bastard Lord Lymm would just love, a command that Fox would hate and attempt to change. He knew when fear—the stick— had to be used and when the carrot might usefully be employed. There came a time when fear would puddle a man's mind, and then he'd be useless to his comrades, to his ship, to his country and—most important of all—to George Abercrombie Fox.

"Bring her around, Kellet. Ease her. Meet her. Steady —steady as you go." Fox lifted his voice. "Mr. Blythe! When your guns bear!"

"Aye aye, sir."

Minion pulled out from the channel, turned through a full half circle and went trudging along parallel to the channel, to the coast, and clear across the Frenchman's stern.

"Rightup him, Mr. Blythe!"

"Aye aye, sir."

Fox had spoken that second injunction to enliven the men. The concept of smashing in the big thirty-two-poun- ders, as it were, up the Frog's backside would appeal to their coarse sense of humor. He saw more than one of the gun crews spit on his hands and rub them together in high good humor.

The activity on the Frenchman and in her boats hauling at bow and stern became frantic.

Grey was beside himself with glee.

"By God, sir! This is a stroke!"

135

"Aye, Mr. Grey. You'll oblige me by making a signal to *Darter* and to the boats to join us. We can compel the Frog to strike between us."

"Aye *aye*, sir."

The signal flags streamed up what was left of *Minion's* mainmast. No answer came from *Darter's* stump mainmast and the boats continued to pull on the ebb down the Roulet. Fox stared back at them and was aware that he could see out of both eyes. He cursed. He waved his fist at *Darter* and then took off that atrocious hat and waved it.

Still *Darter* made no answer and her sweeps drove her down the inlet and towards the open sea.

"They made a mess of it, and now they're leaving us, the bastards!"

Watson harrumphed, but Grey said nothing. In that tiny uncomfortable moment Mr. Blythe's voice rose. "Fire!"

The carronades belched and smoke and flame enwrapped the gun-brig. Fox sniffed the acrid tang of the smoke and he determined that life might be good for him; but when he got back he'd report in to *Boadicea* in terms that would make the officers of *Darter* and the boats think life was a disaster for them. As it damned well should be, confound 'em!

"Come about, Mr. Watson, and we'll put the other broadside into 'em!"

"Aye aye, sir!"

Three times *Minion* punished the sorry frigate. Her boats at her bows were now hauling her around again. Her mizenmast fell. If Fox had enough men—men who were now pulling away from this engagement—he could have boarded and taken the Frenchman. He would have to try to take her on his own and whilst he imagined the English had every chance, it would be a risky business. If only he had a full crew! But that was a pipe-dream in these piping days of war.

Grey yelled.

"Gunboats, sir! Six of 'em. Coming down the inlet!"

Fox sprang onto the ratlines of the mainmast shrouds and looked back. Bigod! There they were. Six flat low gunboats with their oars going like beetles' legs, heading down with the ebb. They'd have twenty-four-pounders mounted in their bows and they'd surround him and blow him to pieces.

CHAPTER TWELVE

His men were few and exhausted. Laboring at the sweeps took all the guts a man had, and the work was laborious in the extreme, despite that Commander Fox changed the hands at frequent intervals. He'd kept his command out of broadside fire from the frigate, and her sternchasers had not hit yet. But with the frigate's turning movements, the six gunboats and the six that followed them down the channel, all able to pull over the shallow water and get at him from all sides, he felt he had no option but to retire.

Fox, being Fox, would not retire gracefully.

"Twelve of them, sir," said Grey. He stood balanced lithely, his young and remarkably handsome face impassive, awaiting the next extraordinary order this extraordinary commander of his would give.

Fox cocked his evil eye up at the flag which, having been shot from the gaff, had subsequently been re-bent twice more in various parts of the rigging. Fox recalled when as a harum-scarum young middy he'd braved maiming and death to rebend the flag at a vital moment. Well, this was a vital moment in an entirely different way. Twelve gun-boats, a frigate, and at least two thirty-sixes firing red-hot shot from the shore fort, or the remains of it. He brushed aside the hot and evil thoughts of what he would like to do to the imbeciles who had blown up the fort without spiking the guns or specifically destroying its equipment.

"So I observe, Mr. Grey," he said. His harsh voice sounded gravelly. By God! He was tired—and tiredness in a sea officer was a mortal sin. "We will go down past the frigate once more and give her a parting shot. Then we will pull after our consorts who signally failed to support us." He glared at Longbridge, the master's mate who had been writing up the slate for later transference to the log. "Have you got all that down, Mr. Longbridge?"

"Aye aye, sir."

Longbridge was a smart young man, who no doubt would not wish to remain in the master's mate rank, notoriously the most difficul to get out of, for very long. "Make sure you note down the time when *Darter* and the boats pulled away against my orders to join with us in taking the frigate."

"Aye aye, sir. All noted down, sir."

Fox grunted and watched as the man at the sweeps pulled and pushed, putting all their bodies' effort into the task. Even then *Minion* crept so slowly through the water it was clear the French gun-boats would be up with her before she was fully out of the mouth of the Roulet.

"Keep 'em at it, Mr. MacMillan!"

"Aye aye, sir!"

The gun-brig pulled away, past the turning stern of the frigate. For the last time her thirty-two-pounder carronades thundered out their power, and the flame gushed and the smoke roiled, and double-shotted they blasted the stern of the Frenchman. Little was left of his stern windows, and the interior of his deck lay open to the day. A tumbled twenty-four-pounder showed, muzzle up, skewed in the splintered wreckage of its port.

"They'll know they've met us, will they," said Fox, getting what satisfaction he could.

That last rolling broadside brought down the Frenchman's mainmast.

The hands set up a cheer. Fox noted with some pleasure that they sounded genuinely pleased, a harsh note of arrogance in the cheer riding over and hiding the exhaustion dragging them all down. Well, they had a long pull ahead of them yet.

Now it was pull, pull, pull, for the open sea.

The french gun-boats swept down on each side of the bedraggled frigate, looking like a swarm of angry bees homing in on their target. Fox walked aft and stood for some time staring at them. Big open boats, they were, with a twenty-four-pounder firmly chocked up in the bows, and with a mass of men aboard. My God, they could crew *Minion*, or near enough, with the crew of one of them. They were coming down fast with the ebb; but Fox guided his command into the deeper channel and took a little direct advantage, for the two center gun-boats kept ahead of their consorts rowing over the shallower water.

"Mr. Grey. Kindly oblige me by laying a carronade aft here. You'll have to work smartly. But—" and here Fox paused, and glared most evilly at Lieutenant Grey. "But do not take foolish risks. I don't want any of the hands hopping about on two smashed ankles."

"Aye aye, sir." And, on the instant, Grey was hammering at the hands to drag a carronade across. It was hard work and the boatswain and carpenter would have to rig fresh belaying points and hook-eyes for the tackle. It might not be worth the trouble. But it would keep an air of activity about his command, the men would see a positive action being taken, and there would be no long-drawn out tension of a stern chase with nothing to do save labor at the sweeps.

Any romantic notions of himself going down and taking a loom and pulling with the men he instantly dispelled. There were men enough for the task, if he rested them properly between stints; his job was to plan and think and to oversee everything that went on.

The fragility of *Minion's* stern, always the weak point in a vessel, would prevent too long or enthusiastic use of the aft carronade. But he fancied a few impressive bangs and clouds of smoke from aft might fractionally deter the two immediately following gun-boats. He'd fight the bastards on his broadsides, and the two six-pounders would have to be aimed forrard to take care of ahead. He had to get this vessel safely down the inlet, not only for *Minion;* but, also, to protect the British boats and *Darter.* Although, given that *Darter* was in much the same case as himself, she could have turned back to his assistance. He was going to be very nasty to Forbes and to the highfalutin' Lieutenant Algernon Faulkner when he got back to *Boadicea,* bigod!

He glared around at the French gun-boats. If he got back. All they had to do was get ahead of him, take up their positions, and blast him with their guns at such a range that his carronades could not reach. The thought spurred him on and he went along the deck, shouting hoarse, jocular, foul words of encouragement to his men. He was aware of their faces turning to him as he passed, their eyes like coals, sizing up this lunatic who had stepped aboard so recently as their new captain. He'd turn 'em into a crew—if he had the chance, if he could get away from these horrible little French gun-boats, like bees, anxious to sting him to death.

The breeze was freshening. No doubt of it. He conjured up in his mind's eye the chart of the Roulet. From landmarks on the bleak shoreline he figured they were well down now, the ebb taking them swiftly through the channel. The frigate was far back now, a lump in the water, to be hidden when they rounded the next curve. Ahead of his own command the lumpy shape of *Darter* was coming into view, with the boats ahead of her. In the event they hadn't had to be towed out. By his actions in going back and taking on the frigate he had given the boats their chance of escape.

The thought occurred to him that they might have seen his action in that light. He brushed it aside. They couldn't be such fools!

He'd had a vessel under him which, although crippled as far as sailing power went, still had a formidable battery of weapons and sweeps for power. No; he'd thrash the stupid truth out of the idiots when he got back.

If he got back.

The left-hand gun-boat astern fired her twenty-four-pounder and the shot skipped into the water alongside. Now they were in for it! The right-hand one fired and her shot, also, skipped into the water. Fox had no need even to glance back to know they were well out of range of his massive carronade.

He stumped about that ridiculous quarterdeck. He looked at the flag, and he vowed that wouldn't come down without a fight, bigod no!

The third shot from astern was followed instantly by an infernal splintering aft and *Minion* shuddered. Grey went calmly below and returned to report the captain's cabin a shambles.

142

"God rot 'em!"

Fox wanted to curse and rave and swing his arms about. He glared balefully back. He had to maintain this careful pose of the cool, calm and collected captain; but he wanted to take those gun-boats and smash 'em to driftwood, every last one. This was his first real command, as a commander, and some French jackals out there were taking her away from him by chopping her to pieces. *Minion* looked now a veritable shambles. He held onto his temper and strolled blockily up and down his silly little quarterdeck.

The next shot missed. Another gun-boat had quartered in and, bringing her bows toward him, had fired, and then resumed her course. That shot missed, too; but soon they'd get the range. He dallied with the idea of abruptly checking his way and belting 'em with his carronades. Yes, by all that was holy, he'd do that—but only when he had enough of 'em under his guns and ready for the chop; he wanted to do damage, did George Abercrombie Fox, he wanted to pay back the hellhounds who were smashing up his very own command.

Odd thoughts tumbled through his head, of that evil swine Captain Stone who had had Fox beaten up by his galley's crew, of that treacherous, sly, overweening enemy of his, Charles Beckworth, Lord Lymm, of the women he had known, the many, many women, and of them all only Sophy Kintlesham sprang to mind with a mist of pink wonder about her face and figure—and what she thought of him now!—and he thought of Swede, and Affleck, of Mr. Midshipman Lunt, and of many others, French and English and all the nationalities who fought in the Royal Navy. Perhaps it was just as well Carker wasn't here. He did not relish the thought of John Carker being shot to pieces along with the rest of them here, and if still alive at the end of the action of being picked off a scrap of floating wreckage to spend the rest of his life in a French prison. They were getting sticky about exchanging prisoners just lately.

More twenty-four-pounder roundshot tore into *Minion*.

She was still not so badly mauled that a dockyard could not repair her. But much more of this and she'd be riddled like a sieve and then they'd break her up for her timber.

"Try a shot aft, Mr. Grey."

Fox spoke grumpily.

"Aye aye, sir."

They both knew the shot would not carry; but the bang and the smoke might hearten the men; in fact, the smoke might for a spell act as a screen.

The carronade let off with its satisfying smack and neither Fox nor Grey bothered to mark the fall of shot.

"Short, sir," sang out Mr. Watson.

"Keep firing," said Fox, in as sour a voice as any he could use. He made up his mind. This was not to be endured. He wasn't going to run away from a pack of measly gun-boats without taking some of them to perdition with him. He glared along his deck. The men were hauling at the sweeps, their bodies bending and straightening with energy, the overall effect one of discipline and power. Most of the wreckage had been cleared away. The gun crews stood to their carronades. He opened his mouth to bellow the order that would bring *Minion* around sharply, to bring all her broadside to bear on the pursuing gun-boats. He yelled, with a viciousness that came, he had to recognize, from despair.

Minion swung to starboard, swiftly, the starboard-side sweeps backing water so that the white scuds spumed.

She swung about with much more spin than she could have managed under sail. The gun-boats following directly

reacted at once and Fox saw their oars frantically splashing in the water as they attempted to back up. They came
down under their own momentum and the ebb just enough
before they began to pull aside.

Fox chuckled. He shouted in a coarse good humor.

"Blow 'em out of the water, Mr. Blythe!"

"Aye aye, sir! As your guns bear! *Fire!*"

The concussions had never sounded sweeter. The
smoke roiled and choked and even as the gun crews went
at their pieces like manicas, Fox bellowed the commands
that brought *Minion* back on course down the Roulet.
The smoke cleared.

A cheer went up. Both the immediately following gun-
boats had gone, scraps of wood floating in the water, and
there were heads of men, bobbling, splashing as they
struck out for their comrades in the adjacent gun-boats.

"Good shooting, Mr. Blythe!"

Then, from forward, a hail, screaming triumphantly
into the breeze.

"Sail ho! Dead ahead! It's *Porcupine* an' *Prosperity!*"

Fox leaped for the ratlines. *Porcupine* and *Prosperity!*
So it was, the two sloops coming into the mouth of the inlet to the rescue. A cheer went up, again, and Fox felt that
at least someone in the British squadron knew an ace from
a deuce. The two sloops could maneuver here, as the
channel widened and the beaches swept back and into
the coastline. The sails came on. Fox looked back. The
gun boats had given up the chase. That might, as well
as being caused by the appearance of two smart British
sloops, be caused also by the nasty chop getting up on the
sea as the wind scoured across the tide. In that kind of sea
the boats would be perfectly good sea-boats; but they'd
have problems with their guns. The sloops could sail
around them and with their six-pounders shatter 'em be-

fore they had a chance to sink their big twenty-four-pounder teeth into the nippy ships.

Minion crawled under her sweeps after *Darter* and the boats.

The two sloops leaned over in the breeze, tacking back to return to the safer open waters beyond . . . Oh, yes, it was enormously pleasant to see those two beautiful little ships, and to know they were commanded by men who wore a swab on their left shoulders, just as Fox did himself.

In his view the night's operations had been a mess. Now he would find out what Captain Dawson might have to say, and he'd have to make damn sure he didn't answer back too much, and speak out of turn, for he dearly relished the feel of that swab, and he wanted to ship it onto his other shoulder, and then ship its mate, and if he stayed out of trouble, why, one day he might do just that, incredible though it might seem for a jumped-up through-the-hawsehole Thames marshboy to dream of such giddy heights.

Here was Grey, actually smiling, lifting his hat.

"Congratulations, sir. A masterly display, if I may say so, sir—"

Fox eyed him. He knew very well what Grey thought of him. He must look a very curious creature to Grey's eyes, and yet they'd caroused and debauched together in Tunbridge Wells. Perhaps that never-admitted friendship could permit a flicker of pleasure now?

"Thank you, Mr. Grey. But there is much to be done before we have a command in which I shall be pleased. I am still awaiting your explanation why that foreroyal was set in so lubberly a fashion."

"Ah, yes, sir—"

"*Boadicea* in sight!" came the hail, and then: "Another frigate with her." A pause in which Fox looked away from

146

Grey. The lookout bellowed again: "Looks like *Meteor*, sir!"

As they waited, still pulling down to the open sea, the list was consulted. Grey looked up, at his captain, and his expression was perfectly unreadable.

"*Meteor*, thirty-two, sir. Captain Lord Lymm."

"A signal from *Meteor*!" came the hail again. Fox made his mind blank. He had to fight against the scarlet arrows of anger and despair that crowded through him. Charles Beckworth, that black bastard, who was now Lord Lymm—what did the blagskite want out here?

"*Meteor's* making our number," said Grey, who was perforce doubling as signals officer.

"Is he bigod," said Fox. "Then he'll have to send a boat for we've none that will swim."

Now the little British squadron clustered in the open sea beyond the mouth of the Roulet. Enemy France lay beyond, and the sea ahead, in which they might find safety until once more they were called upon to deal a blow against Bonaparte. Grey now wore an expression that indicated he was suffering from the most acute indigestion. Everyone else aboard was as lively as one might expect after a successful night action. Fox thought of the opportunities wasted, the men dead, and he began to try to put into words that would not incinerate the paper just what he would say in his report to Captain Dawson.

"Boat coming alongside, sir."

"You'll put on your best uniform, sir?"

"What's that, Mr. Grey? Best uniform?" He thought of that foul peer Lord Lymm, and of his own appearance, and he nodded. Sin had him in its deadly grip. He was bone-weary. "Very well, Mr. Grey. I'll put on a brave front."

For he knew what had happened. It was only too obvious. Captain Dawson of *Boadicea* had been relieved of command and Captain Lymm of *Meteor* had come out to take his place. There would be no joy in the future for Commander Fox.

A strange thought smote Fox. Grey had never served with him under Lymm; so how could it be that Grey, as he so obviously did, could know of the enmity between them? That must be something he must look into. The bow oar hooked onto the main chains. Fox went down into his cabin. Its state made him brace up, and he changed into his fancy new uniform, bought with the loan made him by Staunton, in a new unyielding frame of mind that would see Lord Lymm burn first before he'd give away an inch of that bold front. Back on deck Grey touched his hat to him and they made a bold pretense of seeing their captain over the side, did the crew of *Minion*.

Fox glared at Grey. "We'll be sent back to be patched up, Mr. Grey. And then we'll be back here, poking about these damned Frog inlets again. Next time we won't run with out tails between our legs."

"No, sir. Next time, sir, we'll have a little more fun."

Fox went down into the boat, holding his smart new hat on his head, wondering just what evil barbarity this bastard Lord Lymm had in store for him.

the adventures of
ALEXANDER
SHERIDAN

Exciting front-line action in the mid-1800's —starring one of the toughest professional soldiers ever to bear arms for the Empire!

by V. A. Stuart

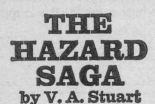